Other titles by Frank B. Linderman
available in Bison Books editions

Henry Plummer
A Novel

Indian Old-*Man Stories*
More Sparks from War Eagle's Lodge-Fire

Kootenai Why Stories

The Montana Stories of Frank B. Linderman

Old Man Coyote

Plenty-Coups
Chief of the Crows

Pretty-Shield
Medicine Woman of the Crows

INDIAN WHY STORIES

SPARKS FROM WAR EAGLE'S LODGE-FIRE

EXPANDED EDITION

FRANK B. LINDERMAN
[CO SKEE SEE CO COT]

Illustrated by Charles M. Russell
[CAH NE TA WAH SEE NA E KET]
The Cowboy Artist

Introduction to the Stories in Verse
by Sarah Waller Hatfield

University of Nebraska Press
Lincoln and London

∞

First Nebraska paperback printing: 2001

Library of Congress Cataloging-in-Publication Data
Linderman, Frank Bird, 1869–1938.
Indian why stories: sparks from War Eagle's lodge-fire /
Frank Linderman (Co skee see co cot); illustrated by
Charles M. Russell (Cah ne ta wah see na e ket), the cowboy
artist; introduction to the stories in verse by Sarah Waller
Hatfield.—Expanded ed.
p.   cm.
ISBN 0-8032-8038-6 (pbk.: alk. paper)
1. Siksika Indians—Folklore.   2. Ojibwa Indians—Folklore.
3. Cree Indians—Folklore.   I. Title.
E99.S54L52   2004
813'.52—dc22   2004010908

I DEDICATE THIS LITTLE BOOK TO MY FRIEND

CHARLES M. RUSSELL
THE COWBOY ARTIST

GEORGE BIRD GRINNELL
THE INDIAN'S FRIEND

AND TO ALL OTHERS WHO HAVE KNOWN AND LOVED OLD MONTANA

FOR I HOLD THEM ALL AS KIN
WHO HAVE BUILDED FIRES WHERE NATURE
WEARS NO MAKE-UP ON HER SKIN

PREFACE

THE great Northwest — that wonderful frontier that called to itself a world's hardiest spirits — is rapidly becoming a settled country; and before the light of civilizing influences, the blanket-Indian has trailed the buffalo over the divide that time has set between the pioneer and the crowd. With his passing we have lost much of the aboriginal folk-lore, rich in its fairy-like characters, and its relation to the lives of a most warlike people.

There is a wide difference between folk-lore of the so-called Old World and that of America. Transmitted orally through countless generations, the folk-stories of our ancestors show many evidences of distortion and of change in material particulars; but the Indian seems to have been too fond of nature and too proud of

PREFACE

tradition to have forgotten or changed the teachings of his forefathers. Childlike in simplicity, beginning with creation itself, and reaching to the whys and wherefores of nature's moods and eccentricities, these tales impress me as being well worth saving.

The Indian has always been a lover of nature and a close observer of her many moods. The habits of the birds and animals, the voices of the winds and waters, the flickering of the shadows, and the mystic radiance of the moonlight — all appealed to him. Gradually, he formulated within himself fanciful reasons for the myriad manifestations of the Mighty Mother and her many children; and a poet by instinct, he framed odd stories with which to convey his explanations to others. And these stories were handed down from father to son, with little variation, through countless generations, until the white man slaughtered the buffalo, took to

PREFACE

himself the open country, and left the red man little better than a beggar. But the tribal story-teller has passed, and only here and there is to be found a patriarch who loves the legends of other days.

Old-man, or Napa, as he is called by the tribes of Blackfeet, is the strangest character in Indian folk-lore. Sometimes he appears as a god or creator, and again as a fool, a thief, or a clown. But to the Indian, Napa is not the Deity; he occupies a somewhat subordinate position, possessing many attributes which have sometimes caused him to be confounded with Manitou, himself. In all of this there is a curious echo of the teachings of the ancient Aryans, whose belief it was that this earth was not the direct handiwork of the Almighty, but of a mere member of a hierarchy of subordinate gods. The Indian possesses the highest veneration for the Great God, who has become familiar to the readers of Indian literature as Manitou. No

PREFACE

idle tales are told of Him, nor would any Indian mention Him irreverently. But with Napa it is entirely different; he appears entitled to no reverence; he is a strange mixture of the fallible human and the powerful under-god. He made many mistakes; was seldom to be trusted; and his works and pranks run from the sublime to the ridiculous. In fact, there are many stories in which Napa figures that will not bear telling at all.

I propose to tell what I know of these legends, keeping as near as possible to the Indian's style of story-telling, and using only tales told me by the older men of the Blackfeet, Chippewa, and Cree tribes.

CONTENTS

CONTENTS

INTRODUCTION

IT was the moon when leaves were falling, for Napa had finished painting them for their dance with the North wind. Just over the ragged mountain range the big moon hung in an almost starless sky, and in shadowy outline every peak lay upon the plain like a giant pattern. Slowly the light spread and as slowly the shadows stole away until the October moon looked down on the great Indian camp — a hundred lodges, each as perfect in design as the tusks of a young silver-tip, and all looking ghostly white in the still of the autumn night.

Back from the camp, keeping within the ever-moving shadows, a buffalo-wolf skulked to a hill overlooking the scene, where he stopped to look and listen, his body silhouetted against the sky. A dog howled occasionally, and the weird sound of a tom-tom accompanying the voice of a singer in the Indian village reached the wolf's ears, but caused him no alarm; for not until a great herd of ponies, under the eyes of the night-herder, drifted too close, did he steal away.

Near the centre of the camp was the big painted lodge of War Eagle, the medicine-man, and inside had gathered his grandchildren, to whom he was telling the stories of the creation and of the strange doings of Napa, the creator. Being a friend of the old historian, I entered unhindered, and with the children listened until the hour grew late, and on the lodge-wall the dying fire made warning shadows dance.

WHY THE CHIPMUNK'S BACK IS
STRIPED

WHY THE CHIPMUNK'S BACK IS STRIPED

WHAT a splendid lodge it was, and how grand War Eagle looked leaning against his back-rest in the firelight! From the tripod that supported the back-rest were suspended his weapons and his medicine-bundle, each showing the wonderful skill of the maker. The quiver that held the arrows was combined with a case for the bow, and colored quills of the porcupine had been deftly used to make it a thing of beauty. All about the lodge hung the strangely painted linings, and the firelight added richness to both color and design. War Eagle's hair was white, for he had known many snows; but his eyes were keen and bright as a boy's, as he gazed in pride at his grandchildren across the lodge-fire. He was wise, and had been in many battles, for his was a

3

warlike tribe. He knew all about the world
and the people in it. He was deeply religious,
and every Indian child loved him for his good-
ness and brave deeds.

About the fire were Little Buffalo Calf, a
boy of eleven years; Eyes-in-the-Water, his
sister, a girl of nine; Fine Bow, a cousin of
these, aged ten, and Bluebird, his sister, who
was but eight years old.

Not a sound did the children make while
the old warrior filled his great pipe, and only
the snapping of the lodge-fire broke the still-
ness. Solemnly War Eagle lit the tobacco
that had been mixed with the dried inner bark
of the red willow, and for several minutes
smoked in silence, while the children's eyes
grew large with expectancy. Finally he spoke:

"Napa, *Old*-man, is very old indeed. He
made this world, and all that is on it. He
came out of the south, and travelled toward
the north, making the birds and animals as
he passed. He made the perfumes for the

4

winds to carry about, and he even made the war-paint for the people to use. He was a busy worker, but a great liar and thief, as I shall show you after I have told you more about him. It was *Old*-man who taught the beaver all his cunning. It was *Old*-man who told the bear to go to sleep when the snow grew deep in winter, and it was he who made the curlew's bill so long and crooked, although it was not that way at first. *Old*-man used to live on this world with the animals and birds. There was no other man or woman then, and he was chief over all the animal-people and the bird-people. He could speak the language of the robin, knew the words of the bear, and understood the sign-talk of the beaver, too. He lived with the wolves, for they are the great hunters. Even to-day we make the same sign for a smart man as we make for the wolf; so you see he taught them much while he lived with them. *Old*-man made a great many mistakes in making things, as I shall show you after a while; yet he worked until he had everything good. But he often made great mischief and taught many wicked things. These I shall tell you about some day. Everybody was afraid of *Old*-man and his tricks and lies — even the animal-people, before he made men and women. He used to visit the lodges of our people and make trouble long ago, but he got so wicked that Manitou grew angry at him, and one day in the month of roses, he built a lodge for *Old*-man and told him that he must stay in it forever. Of course he had to do that, and nobody knows where the lodge was built, nor in what country, but that is why we never see him as our grandfathers did, long, long ago.

"What I shall tell you now happened when the world was young. It was a fine summer day, and *Old*-man was travelling in the forest. He was going north and straight as an arrow — looking at nothing, hearing nothing. No one knows what he was after, to

6

this day. The birds and forest-people spoke politely to him as he passed but he answered none of them. The Pine-squirrel, who is always trying to find out other people's business, asked him where he was going, but *Old*-man wouldn't tell him. The woodpecker hammered on a dead tree to make him look that way, but he wouldn't. The Elk-people and the Deer-people saw him pass, and all said that he must be up to some mischief or he would stop and talk a while. The pine-trees murmured, and the bushes whispered their greeting, but he kept his eyes straight ahead and went on travelling.

"The sun was low when *Old*-man heard a groan" (here War Eagle groaned to show the children how it sounded), "and turning about he saw a warrior lying bruised and bleeding near a spring of cold water. *Old*-man knelt beside the man and asked: 'Is there war in this country?'

"'Yes,' answered the man. 'This whole

day long we have fought to kill a Person, but we have all been killed, I am afraid.'

"'That is strange,' said *Old*-man; 'how can one Person kill so many men? Who is this Person, tell me his name!' but the man didn't answer — he was dead. When *Old*-man saw that life had left the wounded man, he drank from the spring, and went on toward the north, but before long he heard a noise as of men fighting, and he stopped to look and listen. Finally he saw the bushes bend and sway near a creek that flowed through the forest. He crawled toward the spot, and peering through the brush saw a great Person near a pile of dead men, with his back against a pine-tree. The Person was full of arrows, and he was pulling them from his ugly body. Calmly the Person broke the shafts of the arrows, tossed them aside, and stopped the blood flow with a brush of his hairy hand. His head was large and fierce-looking, and his eyes were small and wicked. His great body was larger

8

than that of a buffalo-bull and covered with
scars of many battles.

"*Old*-man went to the creek, and with his
buffalo-horn cup brought some water to the
Person, asking as he approached:

"'Who are you, Person? Tell me, so I
can make you a fine present, for you are great
in war.'

"'I am Bad Sickness,' replied the Person.
'Tribes I have met remember me and always
will, for their bravest warriors are afraid when I
make war upon them. I come in the night or
I visit their camps in daylight. It is always the
same; they are frightened and I kill them easily.'

" 'Ho!' said *Old*-man, 'tell me how to make
Bad Sickness, for I often go to war myself.'
He lied; for he was never in a battle in his life.
The Person shook his ugly head and then *Old*-
man said:

" 'If you will tell me how to make Bad Sickness I will make you small and handsome.
When you are big, as you now are, it is very

9

hard to make a living; but when you are small,
little food will make you fat. Your living
will be easy because I will make your food
grow everywhere.'

" 'Good,' said the Person, 'I will do it;
you must kill the fawns of the deer and the
calves of the elk when they first begin to live.
When you have killed enough of them you
must make a robe of their skins. Whenever
you wear that robe and sing — "now you sicken,
now you sicken," the sickness will come —
that is all there is to it.'

" 'Good,' said *Old*-man, 'now lie down to
sleep and I will do as I promised.'

"The Person went to sleep and *Old*-man
breathed upon him until he grew so tiny that
he laughed to see how small he had made him.
Then he took out his paint sack and striped
the Person's back with black and yellow. It
looked bright and handsome and he waked the
Person, who was now a tiny animal with a
bushy tail to make him pretty.

"'Now,' said *Old*-man, 'you are the Chipmunk, and must always wear those striped clothes. All of your children and their children, must wear them, too.'

"After the Chipmunk had looked at himself, and thanked *Old*-man for his new clothes, he wanted to know how he could make his living, and *Old*-man told him what to eat, and said he must cache the pine-nuts when the leaves turned yellow, so he would not have to work in the winter time.

"'You are a cousin to the Pine-squirrel,' said *Old*-man, 'and you will hunt and hide as he does. You will be spry and your living will be easy to make if you do as I have told you.'

"He taught the Chipmunk his language and his signs, showed him where to live, and then left him, going on toward the north again. He kept looking for the cow-elk and doe-deer, and it was not long before he had killed enough of their young to make the robe as the Person told him, for they were plentiful before the

white man came to live on the world. He
found a shady place near a creek, and there
made the robe that would make Bad Sickness whenever he sang the queer song, but
the robe was plain, and brown in color. He
didn't like the looks of it. Suddenly he thought
how nice the back of the Chipmunk looked
after he had striped it with his paints. He
got out his old paint sack and with the same
colors made the robe look very much like
the clothes of the Chipmunk. He was proud
of the work, and liked the new robe better;
but being lazy, he wanted to save himself
work, so he sent the South-wind to tell all
the doe-deer and the cow-elk to come to him.
They came as soon as they received the message, for they were afraid of *Old*-man and
always tried to please him. When they had
all reached the place where *Old*-man was he
said to them:

"'Do you see this robe?'

"'Yes, we see it,' they replied.

12

"'Well, I have made it from the skins of your children, and then painted it to look like the Chipmunk's back, for I like the looks of that Person's clothes. I shall need many more of these robes during my life; and every time I make one, I don't want to have to spend my time painting it; so from now on and forever your children shall be born in spotted clothes. I want it to be that way to save me work. On all the fawns there must be spots of white like this (here he pointed to the spots on Bad Sickness's robe) and on all of the elk-calves the spots shall not be so white and shall be in rows and look rather yellow.' Again he showed them his robe, that they might see just what he wanted.

"'Remember,' he said, 'after this I don't want to see any of your children running about wearing plain clothing, because that would mean more painting for me. Now go away, and remember what I have said, lest I make you sick.'

"The cow-elk and the doe-deer were glad to know that their children's clothes would be beautiful, and they went away to their little ones who were hidden in the tall grass, where the wolves and mountain-lions would have a hard time finding them; for you know that in the tracks of the fawn there is no scent, and the wolf cannot trail him when he is alone. That is the way Manitou takes care of the weak, and all of the forest-people know about it, too.

"Now you know why the Chipmunk's back is striped, and why the fawn and elk-calf wear their pretty clothes.

"I hear the owls, and it is time for all young men who will some day be great warriors to go to bed, and for all young women to seek rest, lest beauty go away forever. Ho!"

HOW THE DUCKS GOT THEIR FINE FEATHERS

HOW THE DUCKS GOT THEIR FINE FEATHERS

ANOTHER night had come, and I made my way toward War Eagle's lodge. In the bright moonlight the dead leaves of the quaking-aspen fluttered down whenever the wind shook the trees; and over the village great flocks of ducks and geese and swan passed in a never-ending procession, calling to each other in strange tones as they sped away toward the waters that never freeze.

In the lodge War Eagle waited for his grandchildren, and when they had entered, happily, he laid aside his pipe and said:

"The Duck-people are travelling to-night just as they have done since the world was young. They are going away from winter because they cannot make a living when ice covers the rivers.

"You have seen the Duck-people often. You have noticed that they wear fine clothes but you do not know how they got them; so I will tell you to-night.

"It was in the fall when leaves are yellow that it happened, and long, long ago. The Duck-people had gathered to go away, just as they are doing now. The buck-deer was coming down from the high ridges to visit friends in the lowlands along the streams as they have always done. On a lake *Old*-man saw the Duck-people getting ready to go away, and at that time they all looked alike; that is, they all wore the same colored clothes. The loons and the geese and the ducks were there and playing in the sunlight. The loons were laughing loudly and the diving was fast and merry to see. On the hill where *Old*-man stood there was a great deal of moss, and he began to tear it from the ground and roll it into a great ball. When he had gathered all he needed he shouldered the load and started for the shore of

18

the lake, staggering under the weight of the great burden. Finally the Duck-people saw him coming with his load of moss and began to swim away from the shore.

"'Wait, my brothers!' he called, 'I have a big load here, and I am going to give you people a dance. Come and help me get things ready.'

"'Don't you do it,' said the gray goose to the others; 'that's *Old*-man and he is up to something bad, I am sure.'

"So the loon called to *Old*-man and said they wouldn't help him at all.

"Right near the water *Old*-man dropped his ball of moss and then cut twenty long poles. With the poles he built a lodge which he covered with the moss, leaving a doorway facing the lake. Inside the lodge he built a fire and when it grew bright he cried:

"'Say, brothers, why should you treat me this way when I am here to give you a big dance? Come into the lodge,' but they wouldn't do that. Finally *Old*-man began to sing a song in the duck-talk, and keep time with his drum. The Duck-people liked the music, and swam a little nearer to the shore, watching for trouble all the time, but *Old*-man sang so sweetly that pretty soon they waddled up to the lodge and went inside. The loon stopped near the door, for he believed that what the gray goose had said was true, and that *Old*-man was up to some mischief. The gray goose, too, was careful to stay close to the door but the ducks reached all about the fire. Politely, *Old*-man passed the pipe, and they all smoked with him because it is wrong not to smoke in a person's lodge if the pipe is offered, and the Duck-people knew that.

"'Well,' said *Old*-man, 'this is going to be the Blind-dance, but you will have to be painted first.

"'Brother Mallard, name the colors — tell how you want me to paint you.'

"'Well,' replied the mallard drake, 'paint my head green, and put a white circle around my throat, like a necklace. Besides that, I want a brown breast and yellow legs; but I don't want my wife painted that way.'

"*Old*-man painted him just as he asked, and his wife, too. Then the teal and the wood-duck (it took a long time to paint the wood-duck) and the spoonbill and the blue-bill and the canvasback and the goose and the brant and the loon — all chose their paint. *Old*-man painted them all just as they wanted him to, and kept singing all the time. They looked very pretty in the firelight, for it was night before the painting was done.

"'Now,' said *Old*-man, 'as this is the Blind-dance, when I beat upon my drum you must all shut your eyes tight and circle around the fire as I sing. Every one that peeks will have sore eyes forever.'

"Then the Duck-people shut their eyes and *Old*-man began to sing: 'Now you come, ducks, now you come — tum-tum, tum; tum-tum, tum.'

"Around the fire they came with their eyes still shut, and as fast as they reached *Old*-man, the rascal would seize them, and wring their necks. Ho! things were going fine for *Old*-man, but the loon peeked a little, and saw what was going on; several others heard the fluttering and opened their eyes, too. The loon cried out, 'He's killing us — let us fly,' and they did that. There was a great squawking and quacking and fluttering as the Duck-people escaped from the lodge. Ho! but *Old*-man was angry, and he kicked the back of the loon-duck, and that is why his feet turn from his body when he walks or tries to stand. Yes, that is why he is a cripple to-day.

"And all of the Duck-people that peeked that night at the dance still have sore eyes — just as *Old*-man told them they would have. Of course they hurt and smart no more but they stay red to pay for peeking, and always will. You have seen the mallard and the rest of the Duck-people. You can see that the colors *Old*-man painted so long ago are still bright and handsome, and they will stay that way forever and forever. Ho!"

WHY THE KINGFISHER ALWAYS
WEARS A WAR–BONNET

WHY THE KINGFISHER ALWAYS
WEARS A WAR–BONNET

AUTUMN nights on the upper Missouri river in Montana are indescribably beautiful, and under their spell imagination is a constant companion to him who lives in wilderness, lending strange, weird echoes to the voice of man or wolf, and unnatural shapes in shadow to commonplace forms.

The moon had not yet climbed the distant mountain range to look down on the humbler lands when I started for War Eagle's lodge; and dimming the stars in its course, the milky-way stretched across the jewelled sky. "The wolf's trail," the Indians call this filmy streak that foretells fair weather, and to-night it promised much, for it seemed plainer and brighter than ever before.

"How — how!" greeted War Eagle, making

the sign for me to be seated near him, as I entered his lodge. Then he passed me his pipe and together we smoked until the children came.

Entering quietly, they seated themselves in exactly the same positions they had occupied on the previous evenings, and patiently waited in silence. Finally War Eagle laid the pipe away and said: "Ho! Little Buffalo Calf, throw a big stick on the fire and I will tell you why the Kingfisher wears a war-bonnet."

The boy did as he was bidden. The sparks jumped toward the smoke-hole and the blaze lighted up the lodge until it was bright as daytime, when War Eagle continued:

"You have often seen Kingfisher at his fishing along the rivers, I know; and you have heard him laugh in his queer way, for he laughs a good deal when he flies. That same laugh nearly cost him his life once, as you will see. I am sure none could see the Kingfisher without noticing his great head-dress, but not many know how he came by it because it happened so long ago that most men have forgotten.

"It was one day in the winter-time when *Old*-man and the Wolf were hunting. The snow covered the land and ice was on all of the rivers. It was so cold that *Old*-man wrapped his robe close about himself and his breath showed white in the air. Of course the Wolf was not cold; wolves never get cold as men do. Both *Old*-man and the Wolf were hungry for they had travelled far and had killed no meat. *Old*-man was complaining and grumbling, for his heart is not very good. It is never well to grumble when we are doing our best, because it will do no good and makes us weak in our hearts. When our hearts are weak our heads sicken and our strength goes away. Yes, it is bad to grumble.

"When the sun was getting low *Old*-man and the Wolf came to a great river. On the ice that covered the water, they saw four fat Otters playing.

29

"'There is meat,' said the Wolf; 'wait here and I will try to catch one of those fellows.'

"'No!—No!' cried *Old*-man, 'do not run after the Otter on the ice, because there are air-holes in all ice that covers rivers, and you may fall in the water and die.' *Old*-man didn't care much if the Wolf did drown. He was afraid to be left alone and hungry in the snow — that was all.

"'Ho!' said the Wolf, 'I am swift of foot and my teeth are white and sharp. What chance has an Otter against me? Yes, I will go,' and he did.

"Away ran the Otters with the Wolf after them, while *Old*-man stood on the bank and shivered with fright and cold. Of course the Wolf was faster than the Otter, but he was running on the ice, remember, and slipping a good deal. Nearer and nearer ran the Wolf. In fact he was just about to seize an Otter, when SPLASH!—into an air-hole all the Otters went. Ho! the Wolf was going so fast he couldn't stop, and SWOW! into the air-hole he went like a badger after mice, and the current carried him under the ice. The Otters knew that hole was there. That was their country and they were running to reach that same hole all the time, but the Wolf didn't know that.

"*Old*-man saw it all and began to cry and wail as women do. Ho! but he made a great fuss. He ran along the bank of the river, stumbling in the snowdrifts, and crying like a woman whose child is dead; but it was because he didn't want to be left in that country alone that he cried — not because he loved his brother, the Wolf. On and on he ran until he came to a place where the water was too swift to freeze, and there he waited and watched for the Wolf to come out from under the ice, crying and wailing and making an awful noise, for a man.

"Well — right there is where the thing happened. You see, Kingfisher can't fish through

31

the ice and he knows it, too; so he always finds places like the one *Old*-man found. He was there that day, sitting on the limb of a birch-tree, watching for fishes, and when *Old*-man came near to Kingfisher's tree, crying like an old woman, it tickled the Fisher so much that he laughed that queer, chattering laugh.

"*Old*-man heard him and — Ho! but he was angry. He looked about to see who was laughing at him and that made Kingfisher laugh again, longer and louder than before. This time *Old*-man saw him and SWOW! he threw his war-club at Kingfisher; tried to kill the bird for laughing. Kingfisher ducked so quickly that *Old*-man's club just grazed the feathers on his head, making them stand up straight.

"'There,' said *Old*-man, 'I'll teach you to laugh at me when I'm sad. Your feathers are standing up on the top of your head now and they will stay that way, too. As long as you live you must wear a head-dress, to pay for your laughing, and all your children must do the same.

"This was long, long ago, but the Kingfishers have not forgotten, and they all wear war-bonnets, and always will as long as there are Kingfishers.

"Now I will say good night, and when the sun sleeps again I will tell you why the curlew's bill is so long and crooked. Ho!"

WHY THE CURLEW'S BILL IS LONG AND CROOKED

WHY THE CURLEW'S BILL IS LONG AND CROOKED

WHEN we reached War Eagle's lodge we stopped near the door, for the old fellow was singing — singing some old, sad song of younger days and keeping time with his tom-tom. Somehow the music made me sad and not until it had ceased, did we enter.

"How! How!" — he greeted us, with no trace of the sadness in his voice that I detected in his song.

"You have come here to-night to learn why the Curlew's bill is so long and crooked. I will tell you, as I promised, but first I must smoke."

In silence we waited until the pipe was laid aside, then War Eagle began:

"By this time you know that *Old*-man was not always wise, even if he did make the world, and all that is on it. He often got into trouble but something always happened to get him out of it. What I shall tell you now will show you that it is not well to try to do things just because others do them. They may be right for others, and wrong for us, but *Old*-man didn't understand that, you see.

"One day he saw some mice playing and went near to watch them. It was springtime, and the frost was just coming out of the ground. A big flat rock was sticking out of a bank near a creek, and the sun had melted the frost from the earth about it, loosening it, so that it was about to fall. The Chief-Mouse would sing a song, while all the other mice danced, and then the chief would cry 'now!' and all the mice would run past the big rock. On the other side, the Chief-Mouse would sing again, and then say 'now!' — back they would come — right under the dangerous rock. Sometimes little bits of dirt would crumble and fall near the rock, as though

warning the mice that the rock was going to
fall, but they paid no attention to the warning, and kept at their playing. Finally *Old*-
man said:

"'Say, Chief-Mouse, I want to try that.
I want to play that game. I am a good runner.'

"He wasn't, you know, but he thought he
could run. That is often where we make
great mistakes — when we try to do things
we were not intended to do.

"'No — no!' cried the Chief-Mouse, as *Old*-
man prepared to make the race past the rock.
'No! — No! — you will shake the ground.
You are too heavy, and the rock may fall and
kill you. My people are light of foot and
fast. We are having a good time, but if you
should try to do as we are doing you might
get hurt, and that would spoil our fun.'

"'Ho!' said *Old*-man, 'stand back! I'll
show you what a runner I am.'

"He ran like a grizzly bear, and shook the

ground with his weight. Swow! — came the great rock on top of *Old*-man and held him fast in the mud. My! how he screamed and called for aid. All the Mice-people ran away to find help. It was a long time before the Mice-people found anybody, but they finally found the Coyote, and told him what had happened. Coyote didn't like *Old*-man very much, but he said he would go and see what he could do, and he did. The Mice-people showed him the way, and when they all reached the spot — there was *Old*-man deep in the mud, with the big rock on his back. He was angry and was saying things people should not say, for they do no good and make the mind wicked.

"Coyote said: 'Keep still, you big baby. Quit kicking about so. You are splashing mud in my eyes. How can I see with my eyes full of mud? Tell me that. I am going to try to help you out of your trouble.' He tried but *Old*-man insulted Coyote, and called him a name that is not good, so the Coyote said, 'Well, stay there,' and went away.

"Again *Old*-man began to call for helpers, and the Curlew, who was flying over, saw the trouble, and came down to the ground to help. In those days Curlew had a short, stubby bill, and he thought that he could break the rock by pecking it. He pecked and pecked away without making any headway, till *Old*-man grew angry at him, as he did at the Coyote. The harder the Curlew worked, the worse *Old*-man scolded him. *Old*-man lost his temper altogether, you see, which is a bad thing to do, for we lose our friends with it, often. Temper is like a bad dog about a lodge — no friends will come to see us when he is about.

"Curlew did his best but finally said: 'I'll go and try to find somebody else to help you. I guess I am too small and weak. I shall come back to you.' He was standing close to *Old*-man when he spoke, and *Old*-man reached out and grabbed the Curlew by the bill. Curlew began to scream — oh, my — oh, my — oh, my — as you still hear them in the air when it is morning. *Old*-man hung onto the bill and finally pulled it out long and slim, and bent it downward, as it is to-day. Then he let go and laughed at the Curlew.

"'You are a queer-looking bird now. That is a homely bill, but you shall always wear it and so shall all of your children, as long as there are Curlews in the world.'

"I have forgotten who it was that got *Old*-man out of his trouble, but it seems to me it was the bear. Anyhow he did get out somehow, and lived to make trouble, until Manitou grew tired of him.

"There are good things that *Old*-man did and to-morrow night, if you will come early, I will tell you how *Old*-man made the world over after the water made its war on the land, scaring all the animal-people and the bird-people. I will also tell you how he made the first man and the first woman and who they were. But now the grouse is fast asleep; nobody is stirring but those who were made to see in the dark, like the owl and the wolf. — Ho!"

OLD-MAN REMAKES THE WORLD

OLD-MAN REMAKES THE WORLD

THE sun was just sinking behind the hills when we started for War Eagle's lodge.

"To-morrow will be a fine day," said Other-person, "for grandfather says that a red sky is always the sun's promise of fine weather, and the sun cannot lie."

"Yes," said Bluebird, "and he said that when this moon was new it travelled well south for this time of year and its points were up. That means fine, warm weather."

"I wish I knew as much as grandfather," said Fine-bow with pride.

The pipe was laid aside at once upon our entering the lodge and the old warrior said:

"I have told you that *Old*-man taught the animals and the birds all they know. He made them and therefore knew just what each would have to understand in order to make his living. They have never forgotten anything he told them — even to this day. Their grandfathers told the young ones what they had been told, just as I am telling you the things you should know. Be like the birds and animals — tell your children and grandchildren what I have told you, that our people may always know how things were made, and why strange things are true.

"Yes — *Old*-man taught the Beaver how to build his dams to make the water deeper; taught the Squirrel to plant the pine-nut so that another tree might grow and have nuts for his children; told the Bear to go to sleep in the winter, when the snow made hard travelling for his short legs — told him to sleep, and promised him that he would need no meat while he slept. All winter long the Bear sleeps and eats nothing, because *Old*-man told him that he could. He sleeps so much in the winter that he spends most of his time in summer hunting.

"It was *Old*-man who showed the Owl how to hunt at night and it was *Old*-man that taught the Weasel all his wonderful ways — his bloodthirsty ways — for the Weasel is the bravest of the animal-people, considering his size. He taught the Beaver one strange thing that you have noticed, and that is to lay sticks on the creek-bottoms, so that they will stay there as long as he wants them to.

"Whenever the animal-people got into trouble they always sought *Old*-man and told him about it. All were busy working and making a living, when one day it commenced to rain. That was nothing, of course, but it didn't stop as it had always done before. No, it kept right on raining until the rivers over-ran their banks, and the water chased the Weasel out of his hole in the ground. Yes, and it found the Rabbit's hiding-place and made him leave it. It crept into the lodge of the Wolf at night and frightened his wife and children. It poured into the den of the

Bear among the rocks and he had to move. It crawled under the logs in the forest and found the Mice-people. Out it went to the plains and chased them out of their homes in the buffalo skulls. At last the Beavers' dams broke under the strain and that made everything worse. It was bad — very bad, indeed. Everybody except the fish-people were frightened and all went to find *Old*-man that they might tell him what had happened. Finally they found his fire, far up on a timbered bench, and they said that they wanted a council right away.

"It was a strange sight to see the Eagle sitting next to the Grouse; the Rabbit sitting close to the Lynx; the Mouse right under the very nose of the Bobcat, and the tiny Humming-bird talking to the Hawk in a whisper, as though they had always been great friends. All about *Old*-man's fire they sat and whispered or talked in signs. Even the Deer spoke to the Mountain-lion, and the Antelope told the

Wolf that he was glad to see him, because fear had made them all friends.

"The whispering and the sign-making stopped when *Old*-man raised his hand — like that" (here War Eagle raised his hand with the palm outward) — "and asked them what was troubling them.

"The Bear spoke first, of course, and told how the water had made him move his camp. He said all the animal-people were moving their homes, and he was afraid they would be unable to find good camping-places, because of the water. Then the Beaver spoke, because he is wise and all the forest-people know it. He said his dams would not hold back the water that came against them; that the whole world was a lake, and that he thought they were on an island. He said he could live in the water longer than most people, but that as far as he could see they would all die except, perhaps, the fish-people, who stayed in the water all the time, anyhow. He said he couldn't think of a thing to do — then he sat down and the sign-talking and whispering commenced again.

"*Old*-man smoked a long time — smoked and thought hard. Finally he grabbed his magic stone axe, and began to sing his war-song. Then the rest knew he had made up his mind and knew what he would do. Swow! he struck a mighty pine-tree a blow, and it fell down. Swow! down went another and another, until he had ten times ten of the longest, straightest, and largest trees in all the world lying side by side before him. Then *Old*-man chopped off the limbs, and with the aid of magic rolled the great logs tight together. With withes of willow that he told the Beaver to cut for him, he bound the logs fast together until they were all as one. It was a monstrous raft that *Old*-man had built, as he sang his song in the darkness. At last he cried, 'Ho! everybody hurry and sit on this raft I have made'; and they did hurry.

"It was not long till the water had reached the logs; then it crept in between them, and finally it went on past the raft and off into the forest, looking for more trouble.

"By and by the raft began to groan, and the willow withes squeaked and cried out as though ghost-people were crying in the night. That was when the great logs began to tremble as the water lifted them from the ground. Rain was falling — night was there, and fear made cowards of the bravest on the raft. All through the forest there were bad noises — noises that make the heart cold — as the raft bumped against great trees rising from the earth that they were leaving forever.

"Higher and higher went the raft; higher than the bushes; higher than the limbs on the trees; higher than the Woodpecker's nest; higher than the tree tops, and even higher than the mountains. Then the world was no more, for the water had whipped the land in the war it made against it.

"Day came, and still the rain was falling. Night returned, and yet the rain came down. For many days and nights they drifted in the falling rain; whirling and twisting about while the water played with the great raft, as a Bear would play with a Mouse. It was bad, and they were all afraid — even *Old*-man himself was scared.

"At last the sun came but there was no land. All was water. The water was the world. It reached even to the sky and touched it all about the edges. All were hungry, and some of them were grumbling, too. There are always grumblers when there is great trouble, but they are not the ones who become great chiefs — ever.

"*Old*-man sat in the middle of the raft and thought. He knew that something must be done, but he didn't know what. Finally he said: 'Ho! Chipmunk, bring me the Spotted Loon. Tell him I want him.'

"The Chipmunk found the Spotted Loon

and told him that *Old*-man wanted him, so the Loon went to where *Old*-man sat. When he got there, *Old*-man said:

"'Spotted Loon you are a great diver. Nobody can dive as you can. I made you that way and I know. If you will dive and swim down to the world I think you might bring me some of the dirt that it is made of — then I am sure I can make another world.'

"'It is too deep, this water,' replied the Loon, 'I am afraid I shall drown.'

"'Well, what if you do?' said *Old*-man. 'I gave you life, and if you lose it this way I will return it to you. You shall live again!'

"'All right, *Old*-man,' he answered, 'I am willing to try'; so he waddled to the edge of the raft. He is a poor walker — the Loon, and you know I told you why. It was all because *Old*-man kicked him in the back the night he painted all the Duck-people.

"Down went the Spotted Loon, and long he stayed beneath the water. All waited and watched, and longed for good luck, but when he came to the top he was dead. Everybody groaned — all felt badly, I can tell you, as *Old*-man laid the dead Loon on the logs. The Loon's wife was crying, but *Old*-man told her to shut up and she did.

"Then *Old*-man blew his own breath into the Loon's bill, and he came back to life.

"'What did you see, Brother Loon?' asked *Old*-man, while everybody crowded as close as he could.

"'Nothing but water,' answered the Loon, 'we shall all die here, I cannot reach the world by swimming. My heart stops working.'

"There were many brave ones on the raft, and the Otter tried to reach the world by diving; and the Beaver, and the Gray Goose, and the Gray Goose's wife; but all died in trying, and all were given a new life by *Old*-man. Things were bad and getting worse. Everybody was cross, and all wondered what *Old*-man would do next, when somebody laughed.

"All turned to see what there could be to laugh at, at such a time, and *Old*-man turned about just in time to see the Muskrat bid good-by to his wife — that was what they were laughing at. But he paid no attention to *Old*-man or the rest, and slipped from the raft to the water. Flip! — his tail cut the water like a knife, and he was gone. Some laughed again, but all wondered at his daring, and waited with little hope in their hearts; for the Muskrat wasn't very great, they thought.

"He was gone longer than the Loon, longer than the Beaver, longer than the Otter or the Gray Goose or his wife, but when he came to the surface of the water he was dead.

"*Old*-man brought Muskrat back to life, and asked him what he had seen on his journey. Muskrat said: 'I saw trees, *Old*-man, but I died before I got to them.'

"*Old*-man told him he was brave. He said

57

his people should forever be great if he succeeded in bringing some dirt to the raft; so just as soon as the Muskrat was rested he dove again.

"When he came up he was dead, but clinched in his tiny hand *Old*-man found some dirt — not much, but a little. A second time *Old*-man gave the Muskrat his breath, and told him that he must go once more, and bring dirt. He said there was not quite enough in the first lot, so after resting a while the Muskrat tried a third time and a third time he died, but brought up a little more dirt.

"Everybody on the raft was anxious now, and they were all crowding about *Old*-man; but he told them to stand back, and they did. Then he blew his breath in Muskrat's mouth a third time, and a third time he lived and joined his wife.

"*Old*-man then dried the dirt in his hands, rubbing it slowly and singing a queer song. Finally it was dry; then he settled the hand that held the dirt in the water slowly, until the water touched the dirt. The dry dirt began to whirl about and then *Old*-man blew upon it. Hard he blew and waved his hands, and the dirt began to grow in size right before their eyes. *Old*-man kept blowing and waving his hands until the dirt became real land, and the trees began to grow. So large it grew that none could see across it. Then he stopped his blowing and sang some more. Everybody wanted to get off the raft, but *Old*-man said 'no.'

"'Come here, Wolf,' he said, and the Wolf came to him.

"'You are swift of foot and brave. Run around this land I have made, that I may know how large it is.'

"The Wolf started, and it took him half a year to get back to the raft. He was very poor from much running, too, but *Old*-man said the world wasn't big enough yet so he blew some more, and again sent the Wolf out

to run around the land. He never came back
— no, the *Old*-man had made it so big that the
Wolf died of old age before he got back to the
raft. Then all the people went out upon the
land to make their living, and they were
happy, there, too.

"After they had been on the land for a long
time *Old*-man said: 'Now I shall make a man
and a woman, for I am lonesome living with
you people. He took two or three handfuls
of mud from the world he had made, and
moulded both a man and a woman. Then he
set them side by side and breathed upon them.
They lived! — and he made them very strong
and healthy — very beautiful to look upon.
Chippewas, he called these people, and they
lived happily on that world until a white man
saw an Eagle sailing over the land and came to
look about. He stole the woman — that white
man did; and that is where all the tribes came
from that we know to-day. None are pure of
blood but the two humans he made of clay,

and their own children. And they are the Chippewas!

"That is a long story and now you must hurry to bed. To-morrow night I will tell you another story — Ho!"

WHY BLACKFEET NEVER KILL MICE

WHY BLACKFEET NEVER KILL MICE

MUSKRAT and his grandmother were gathering wood for the camp the next morning, when they came to an old buffalo skull. The plains were dotted with these relics of the chase, for already the hide-hunting white man had played havoc with the great herds of buffalo. This skull was in a grove of cottonwood-trees near the river, and as they approached two Mice scampered into it to hide. Muskrat, in great glee, secured a stick and was about to turn the skull over and kill the Mice, when his grandmother said: "No, our people never kill Mice. Your grandfather will tell you why if you ask him. The Mice-people are our friends and we treat them as such. Even small people can be good friends, you know — remember that."

All the day the boy wondered why the Mice-people should not be harmed; and just at dark he came for me to accompany him to War Eagle's lodge. On the way he told me what his grandmother had said, and that he intended to ask for the reason, as soon as we arrived. We found the other children already there, and almost before we had seated ourselves, Muskrat asked:

"Grandfather, why must we never kill the Mice-people? Grandmother said that you knew."

"Yes," replied War Eagle, "I do know and you must know. Therefore I shall tell you all to-night why the Mice-people must be let alone and allowed to do as they please, for we owe them much; much more than we can ever pay. Yes — they are great people, as you will see.

"It happened long, long ago, when there were few men and women on the world. *Old-*man was chief of all then, and the animal-people and the bird-people were greater than our people, because we had not been on earth long and were not wise.

"There was much quarrelling among the animals and the birds. You see the Bear wanted to be chief, under *Old*-man, and so did the Beaver. Almost every night they would have a council and quarrel over it. Beside the Bear and Beaver, there were other animals, and also birds, that thought they had the right to be chief. They couldn't agree and the quarrelling grew worse as time went on. Some said the greatest thief should be chosen. Others thought the wisest one should be the leader; while some said the swiftest traveller was the one they wanted. So it went on and on until they were most all enemies instead of friends, and you could hear them quarrelling almost every night, until *Old*-man came along that way.

"He heard about the trouble. I forget who told him, but I think it was the Rabbit. Anyhow he visited the council where the quarrelling was going on and listened to what each one had to say. It took until almost daylight, too. He listened to it all — every bit. When they had finished talking and the quarrelling commenced as usual, he said, 'stop!' and they did stop.

"Then he said to them: 'I will settle this thing right here and right now, so that there will be no more rows over it, forever.'

"He opened his paint sack and took from it a small, polished bone. This he held up in the firelight, so that they might all see it, and he said:

"'This will settle the quarrel. You all see this bone in my right hand, don't you?'

"'Yes,' they replied.

"'Well, now you watch the bone and my hands, too, for they are quick and cunning.'

"*Old*-man began to sing the gambling song and to slip the bone from one hand to the other so rapidly and smoothly that they were all puzzled. Finally he stopped singing and held

68

out his hands — both shut tight, and both with their backs up.

"'Which of my hands holds the bone now?' he asked them.

"Some said it was in the right hand and others claimed that it was the left hand that held it. *Old*-man asked the Bear to name the hand that held the bone, and the Bear did; but when *Old*-man opened that hand it was empty — the bone was not there. Then everybody laughed at the Bear. *Old*-man smiled a little and began to sing and again pass the bone.

"'Beaver, you are smart; name the hand that holds the bone this time.'

"The Beaver said: 'It's in your right hand. I saw you put it there.'

"*Old*-man opened that hand right before the Beaver's eyes, but the bone wasn't there, and again everybody laughed — especially the Bear.

"'Now, you see,' said *Old*-man, 'that this

is not so easy as it looks, but I am going to teach you all to play the game; and when you have all learned it, you must play it until you find out who is the cleverest at the playing. Whoever that is, he shall be chief under me, forever.'

"Some were awkward and said they didn't care much who was chief, but most all of them learned to play pretty well. First the Bear and the Beaver tried it, but the Beaver beat the Bear easily and held the bone for ever so long. Finally the Buffalo beat the Beaver and started to play with the Mouse. Of course the Mouse had small hands and was quicker than the Buffalo — quicker to see the bone. The Buffalo tried hard for he didn't want the Mouse to be chief but it didn't do him any good; for the Mouse won in the end.

"It was a fair game and the Mouse was chief under the agreement. He looked quite small among the rest but he walked right out to the centre of the council and said:

"'Listen, brothers — what is mine to keep is mine to give away. I am too small to be your chief and I know it. I am not warlike. I want to live in peace with my wife and family. I know nothing of war. I get my living easily. I don't like to have enemies. I am going to give my right to be chief to the man that *Old*-man has made like himself.'

"That settled it. That made the man chief forever, and that is why he is greater than the animals and the birds. That is why we never kill the Mice-people.

"You saw the Mice run into the buffalo skull, of course. There is where they have lived and brought up their families ever since the night the Mouse beat the Buffalo playing the bone game. Yes — the Mice-people always make their nests in the heads of the dead Buffalo-people, ever since that night.

"Our people play the same game, even today. See," and War Eagle took from his paint sack a small, polished bone. Then he sang just as *Old*-man did so long ago. He let the children try to guess the hand that held the bone, as the animal-people did that fateful night; but, like the animals, they always guessed wrong. Laughingly War Eagle said:

"Now go to your beds and come to see me to-morrow night. Ho!"

HOW THE OTTER SKIN BECAME
GREAT "MEDICINE"

HOW THE OTTER SKIN BECAME
GREAT "MEDICINE"

IT was rather late when we left War Eagle's lodge after having learned why the Indians never kill the Mice-people; and the milky way was white and plain, dimming the stars with its mist. The children all stopped to say good night to little Sees-in-the-dark, a brand-new baby sister of Bluebird's; then they all went to bed.

The next day the boys played at war, just as white boys do; and the girls played with dolls dressed in buckskin clothes, until it grew tiresome, when they visited relatives until it came time for us all to go to their grand-father's lodge. He was smoking when we entered, but soon laid aside the pipe and said:

"You know that the otter skin is big medi-cine, no doubt. You have noticed that our

warriors wear it sometimes and you know
that we all think it very lucky to wear the
skin of the Otter. But you don't know how
it came to be great; so I shall tell you.

"One time, long before my grandfather was
born, a young-man of our tribe was unlucky
in everything. No woman wanted to marry
him, because he couldn't kill enough meat to
keep her in food and clothes. Whenever he
went hunting, his bow always broke or he
would lose his lance. If these things didn't
happen, his horse would fall and hurt him.
Everybody talked about him and his bad
luck, and although he was fine-looking, he
had no close friends, because of his ill fortune.
He tried to dream and get his medicine but
no dream would come. He grew sour and
people were sorry for him all the time. Finally
his name was changed to 'The Unlucky-one,'
which sounds bad to the ear. He used to
wander about alone a good deal, and one
morning he saw an old woman gathering wood

by the side of a river. The Unlucky-one was about to pass the old woman when she stopped him and asked:

"'Why are you so sad in your handsome face? Why is that sorry look in your fine eyes?'

"'Because,' replied the young-man, 'I am the Unlucky-one. Everything goes wrong with me, always. I don't want to live any longer, for my heart is growing wicked.'

"'Come with me,' said the old woman, and he followed her until she told him to sit down. Then she said: 'Listen to me. First you must learn a song to sing, and this is it.' Then she sang a queer song over and over again until the young-man had learned it well.

"'Now do what I tell you, and your heart shall be glad some day.' She drew from her robe a pair of moccasins and a small sack of dried meat. 'Here,' she said, 'put these moccasins on your feet and take this sack of

meat for food, for you must travel far. Go
on down this river until you come to a great
beaver village. Their lodges will be large and
fine-looking and you will know the village by
the great size of the lodges. When you get
to the place, you must stand still for a long
time, and then sing the song I taught you.
When you have finished the singing, a great
white Beaver, chief of all the Beavers in the
world, will come to you. He is wise and can
tell you what to do to change your luck. After
that I cannot help you; but do what the white
Beaver tells you, without asking why. Now
go, and be brave!'

"The young-man started at once. Long
his steps were, for he was young and strong.
Far he travelled down the river — saw many
beaver villages, too, but he did not stop, because the lodges were not big, as the old woman
told him they would be in the right village.
His feet grew tired for he travelled day and
night without resting, but his heart was brave

and he believed what the old woman had told him.

"It was late on the third day when he came to a mighty beaver village and here the lodges were greater than any he had ever seen before. In the centre of the camp was a monstrous lodge built of great sticks and towering above the rest. All about, the ground was neat and clean and bare as your hand. The Unlucky-one knew this was the white Beaver's lodge — knew that at last he had found the chief of all the Beavers in the world; so he stood still for a long time, and then sang that song.

"Soon a great white Beaver — white as the snows of winter — came to him and asked: 'Why do you sing that song, my brother? What do you want of me? I have never heard a man sing that song before. You must be in trouble.'

"'I am the Unlucky-one,' the young-man replied. 'I can do nothing well. I can find no woman who will marry me. In the hunt my bow will often break or my lance is poor. My medicine is bad and I cannot dream. The people do not love me, and they pity me as they do a sick child.'

"'I am sorry for you,' said the white Beaver — chief of all the Beavers in the world — 'but you must find my brother the Coyote, who knows where *Old*-man's lodge is. The Coyote will do your bidding if you sing that song when you see him. Take this stick with you, because you will have a long journey, and with the stick you may cross any river and not drown, if you keep it always in your hand. That is all I can do for you, myself.'

"On down the river the Unlucky-one travelled and the sun was low in the west on the fourth day, when he saw the Coyote on a hillside near by. After looking at Coyote for a long time, the young-man commenced to sing the song the old woman had taught him. When he had finished the singing, the Coyote came up close and asked:

"'What is the matter? Why do you sing that song? I never heard a man sing it before. What is it you want of me?'

"Then the Unlucky-one told the Coyote what he had told the white Beaver, and showed the stick the Beaver-chief had given him, to prove it.

"'I am hungry, too,' said the Unlucky-one, 'for I have eaten all the dried meat the old woman gave me.'

"'Wait here,' said the Coyote, 'my brother the Wolf has just killed a fat Doe, and perhaps he will give me a little of the meat when I tell him about you and your troubles.'

"Away went the Coyote to beg for meat, and while he was gone the young-man bathed his tired feet in a cool creek. Soon the Coyote came back with meat, and young-man built a fire and ate some of it, even before it was warm, for he was starving. When he had finished the Coyote said:

"'Now I shall take you to *Old*-man's lodge, come.'

"They started, even though it was getting dark. Long they travelled without stopping — over plains and mountains — through great forests and across rivers, until they came to a cave in the rough rocks on the side of a mighty mountain.

"'In there,' said the Coyote, 'you will find *Old*-man and he can tell you what you want to know.'

"The Unlucky-one stood before the black hole in the rocks for a long time, because he was afraid; but when he turned to speak to the Coyote he found himself to be alone. The Coyote had gone about his own business — had silently slipped away in the night.

"Slowly and carefully the young-man began to creep into the cave, feeling his way in the darkness. His heart was beating like a tom-tom at a dance. Finally he saw a fire away back in the cave.

"The shadows danced about the stone sides of the cave as men say the ghosts do; and they frightened him. But looking, he saw a man sitting on the far side of the fire. The man's hair was like the snow and very long. His face was wrinkled with the seams left by many years of life and he was naked in the firelight that played about him.

"Slowly the young-man stood upon his feet and began to walk toward the fire with great fear in his heart. When he had reached the place where the firelight fell upon him, the *Old*-man looked up and said:

"'How, young-man, I am *Old*-man. Why did you come here? What is it you want?'

"Then the Unlucky-one told *Old*-man just what he had told the old woman and the white Beaver and the Coyote, and showed the stick the Beaver had given him, to prove it.

"'Smoke,' said *Old*-man, and passed the pipe to his visitor. After they had smoked *Old*-man said:

"'I will tell you what to do. On the top of this great mountain there live many ghost-

people and their chief is a great Owl. This
Owl is the only one who knows how you can
change your luck, and he will tell you if you
are not afraid. Take this arrow and go among
those people, without fear. Show them you
are unarmed as soon as they see you. Now
go!'

"Out into the night went the Unlucky-one
and on up the mountain. The way was rough
and the wind blew from the north, chilling his
limbs and stinging his face, but on he went
toward the mountain-top, where the storm-
clouds sleep and the winter always stays.
Drifts of snow were piled all about, and the
wind gathered it up and hurled it at the young-
man as though it were angry at him. The
clouds waked and gathered around him, making
the night darker and the world lonelier than
before, but on the very top of the mountain
he stopped and tried to look through the
clouds. Then he heard strange singing all
about him; but for a long time there was no

singer in sight. Finally the clouds parted
and he saw a great circle of ghost-people with
large and ugly heads. They were seated on
the icy ground and on the drifts of snow and
on the rocks, singing a warlike song that made
the heart of the young-man stand still, in
dread. In the centre of the circle there sat
a mighty Owl — their chief. Ho! — when the
ghost-people saw the Unlucky-one they rushed
at him with many lances and would have killed
him but the Owl-chief cried, 'Stop!'

"The young-man folded his arms and said:
'I am unarmed — come and see how a Blackfoot dies. I am not afraid of you.'

"'Ho!' said the Owl-chief, 'we kill no unarmed man. Sit down, my son, and tell me
what you want. Why do you come here?
You must be in trouble. You must smoke
with me.'

"The Unlucky-one told the Owl-chief just
what he had told the old woman and the Beaver
and the Coyote and *Old*-man, and showed the

stick that the white Beaver had given him and the arrow that *Old*-man had given to him to prove it.

"'Good,' said the Owl-chief, 'I can help you, but first you must help yourself. Take this bow. It is a medicine-bow; then you will have a bow that will not break and an arrow that is good and straight. Now go down this mountain until you come to a river. It will be dark when you reach this river, but you will know the way. There will be a great cottonwood-tree on the bank of the stream where you first come to the water. At this tree, you must turn down the stream and keep on travelling without rest, until you hear a splashing in the water near you. When you hear the splashing, you must shoot this arrow at the sound. Shoot quickly, for if you do not you can never have any good luck. If you do as I have told you the splasher will be killed and you must then take his hide and wear it always. The skin that the splasher wears will make you a lucky man. It will make anybody lucky and you may tell your people that it is so.

"'Now go, for it is nearly day and we must sleep.'

"The young-man took his bow and arrow and the stick the white Beaver had given him and started on his journey. All the day he travelled, and far into the night. At last he came to a river and on the bank he saw the great cottonwood-tree, just as the ghost Owl had told him. At the tree the young-man turned down the stream and in the dark easily found his way along the bank. Very soon he heard a great splashing in the water near him, and — zipp — he let the arrow go at the sound — then all was still again. He stood and looked and listened, but for a long time could see nothing — hear nothing.

"Then the moon came out from under a cloud and just where her light struck the river, he saw some animal floating — dead.

87

With the magic stick the young-man walked out on the water, seized the animal by the legs and drew it ashore. It was an Otter, and the young-man took his hide, right there.

"A Wolf waited in the brush for the body of the Otter, and the young-man gave it to him willingly, because he remembered the meat the Wolf had given the Coyote. As soon as the young-man had skinned the Otter he threw the hide over his shoulder and started for his own country with a light heart, but at the first good place he made a camp, and slept. That night he dreamed and all was well with him.

"After days of travel he found his tribe again, and told what had happened. He became a great hunter and a great chief among us. He married the most beautiful woman in the tribe and was good to her always. They had many children, and we remember his name as one that was great in war. That is all — Ho!"

OLD–MAN STEALS THE SUN'S
LEGGINGS

OLD-MAN STEALS THE SUN'S
LEGGINGS

FIRELIGHT — what a charm it adds to story-telling. How its moods seem to keep pace with situations pictured by the oracle, offering shadows when dread is abroad, and light when a pleasing climax is reached; for interest undoubtedly tends the blaze, while sympathy contributes or withholds fuel, according to its dictates.

The lodge was alight when I approached and I could hear the children singing in a happy mood, but upon entering, the singing ceased and embarrassed smiles on the young faces greeted me; nor could I coax a continuation of the song.

Seated beside War Eagle was a very old Indian whose name was Red Robe, and as soon as I was seated, the host explained that he was an honored guest; that he was a Sioux and a friend of long standing. Then War Eagle lighted the pipe, passing it to the distinguished friend, who in turn passed it to me, after first offering it to the Sun, the father, and the Earth, the mother of all that is.

In a lodge of the Blackfeet the pipe must never be passed across the doorway. To do so would insult the host and bring bad luck to all who assembled. Therefore if there be a large number of guests ranged about the lodge, the pipe is passed first to the left from guest to guest until it reaches the door, when it goes back, unsmoked, to the host, to be refilled ere it is passed to those on his right hand.

Briefly War Eagle explained my presence to Red Robe and said:

"Once the Moon made the Sun a pair of leggings. Such beautiful work had never been seen before. They were worked with the colored quills of the Porcupine and were covered with strange signs, which none but the Sun and the Moon could read. No man ever saw such leggings as they were, and it took the Moon many snows to make them. Yes, they were wonderful leggings and the Sun always wore them on fine days, for they were bright to look upon.

"Every night when the Sun went to sleep in his lodge away in the west, he used the leggings for a pillow, because there was a thief in the world, even then. That thief and rascal was *Old*-man, and of course the Sun knew all about him. That is why he always put his fine leggings under his head when he slept. When he worked he almost always wore them, as I have told you, so that there was no danger of losing them in the daytime; but the Sun was careful of his leggings when night came and he slept.

"You wouldn't think that a person would be so foolish as to steal from the Sun, but one night *Old*-man — who is the only person who ever knew just where the Sun's lodge was — crept near enough to look in, and saw the leggings under the Sun's head.

"We have all travelled a great deal but no man ever found the Sun's lodge. No man knows in what country it is. Of course we know it is located somewhere west of here, for we see him going that way every afternoon, but *Old*-man knew everything — except that he could not fool the Sun.

"Yes — *Old*-man looked into the lodge of the Sun and saw the leggings there — saw the Sun, too, and the Sun was asleep. He made up his mind that he would steal the leggings so he crept through the door of the lodge. There was no one at home but the Sun, for the Moon has work to do at night just as the children, the Stars, do, so he thought he could slip the leggings from under the sleeper's head and get away.

"He got down on his hands and knees to walk like the Bear-people and crept into the lodge, but in the black darkness he put his knee upon a dry stick near the Sun's bed. The stick snapped under his weight with so great a noise that the Sun turned over and snorted, scaring *Old*-man so badly that he couldn't move for a minute. His heart was not strong — wickedness makes every heart weaker — and after making sure that the Sun had not seen him, he crept silently out of the lodge and ran away.

"On the top of a hill *Old*-man stopped to look and listen, but all was still; so he sat down and thought.

"'I'll get them to-morrow night when he sleeps again'; he said to himself. 'I need those leggings myself, and I'm going to get them, because they will make me handsome as the Sun.'

"He watched the Moon come home to camp and saw the Sun go to work, but he did not go very far away because he wanted to be near the lodge when night came again.

"It was not long to wait, for all the *Old*-man had to do was to make mischief, and only those who have work to do measure time. He was close to the lodge when the Moon came out, and there he waited until the Sun went inside. From the bushes *Old*-man saw the Sun take off his leggings and his eyes glittered with greed as he saw their owner fold them and put them under his head as he had always done. Then he waited a while before creeping closer. Little by little the old rascal crawled toward the lodge, till finally his head was inside the door. Then he waited a long, long time, even after the Sun was snoring.

"The strange noises of the night bothered him, for he knew he was doing wrong, and when a Loon cried on a lake near by, he shivered as with cold, but finally crept to the sleeper's side. Cautiously his fingers felt about the precious leggings until he knew just how they could best be removed without waking the

Sun. His breath was short and his heart was beating as a war-drum beats, in the black dark of the lodge. Sweat — cold sweat, that great fear always brings to the weak-hearted — was dripping from his body, and once he thought that he would wait for another night, but greed whispered again, and listening to its voice, he stole the leggings from under the Sun's head.

"Carefully he crept out of the lodge, looking over his shoulder as he went through the door. Then he ran away as fast as he could go. Over hills and valleys, across rivers and creeks, toward the east. He wasted much breath laughing at his smartness as he ran, and soon he grew tired.

"'Ho!' he said to himself, 'I am far enough now and I shall sleep. It's easy to steal from the Sun — just as easy as stealing from the Bear or the Beaver.'

"He folded the leggings and put them under his head as the Sun had done, and went to sleep. He had a dream and it waked him with a start. Bad deeds bring bad dreams to us all. *Old*-man sat up and there was the Sun looking right in his face and laughing. He was frightened and ran away, leaving the leggings behind him.

"Laughingly the Sun put on the leggings and went on toward the west, for he is always busy. He thought he would see *Old*-man no more, but it takes more than one lesson to teach a fool to be wise, and *Old*-man hid in the timber until the Sun had travelled out of sight. Then he ran westward and hid himself near the Sun's lodge again, intending to wait for the night and steal the leggings a second time.

"He was much afraid this time, but as soon as the Sun was asleep he crept to the lodge and peeked inside. Here he stopped and looked about, for he was afraid the Sun would hear his heart beating. Finally he started toward the Sun's bed and just then a great white

Owl flew from off the lodge poles, and this scared him more, for that is very bad luck and he knew it; but he kept on creeping until he could almost touch the Sun.

"All about the lodge were beautiful linings, tanned and painted by the Moon, and the queer signs on them made the old coward tremble. He heard a night-bird call outside and he thought it would surely wake the Sun; so he hastened to the bed and with cunning fingers stole the leggings, as he had done the night before, without waking the great sleeper. Then he crept out of the lodge, talking bravely to himself as cowards do when they are afraid.

"'Now,' he said to himself, 'I shall run faster and farther than before. I shall not stop running while the night lasts, and I shall stay in the mountains all the time when the Sun is at work in the daytime!'

"Away he went — running as the Buffalo runs — straight ahead, looking at nothing, hearing nothing, stopping at nothing. When

day began to break *Old*-man was far from
the Sun's lodge and he hid himself in a deep
gulch among some bushes that grew there.
He listened a long time before he dared to go
to sleep, but finally he did. He was tired
from his great run and slept soundly and for a
long time, but when he opened his eyes —
there was the Sun looking straight at him,
and this time he was scowling. *Old*-man
started to run away but the Sun grabbed
him and threw him down upon his back.
My! but the Sun was angry, and he said:

"'*Old*-man, you are a clever thief but a
mighty fool as well, for you steal from me and
expect to hide away. Twice you have stolen
the leggings my wife made for me, and twice
I have found you easily. Don't you know
that the whole world is my lodge and that
you can never get outside of it, if you run
your foolish legs off? Don't you know that
I light all of my lodge every day and search
it carefully? Don't you know that nothing

can hide from me and live? I shall not harm you this time, but I warn you now, that if you ever steal from me again, I will hurt you badly. Now go, and don't let me catch you stealing again!'

"Away went *Old*-man, and on toward the west went the busy Sun. That is all.

"Now go to bed; for I would talk of other things with my friend, who knows of war as I do. Ho!"

OLD–MAN AND HIS CONSCIENCE

OLD-MAN AND HIS CONSCIENCE

NOT so many miles away from the village, the great mountain range so divides the streams that are born there, that their waters are offered as tribute to the Atlantic, Pacific, and Arctic Oceans. In this wonderful range the Indians believe the winds are made, and that they battle for supremacy over Gunsight Pass. I have heard an old story, too, that is said to have been generally believed by the Blackfeet, in which a monster bull-elk that lives in Gunsight Pass lords it over the winds. This elk creates the North wind by "flapping" one of his ears, and the South wind by the same use of his other. I am inclined to believe that the winds are made in that Pass, myself, for there they are seldom at rest, especially at this season of the year.

To-night the wind was blowing from the north, and filmy white clouds were driven across the face of the nearly full moon, momentarily veiling her light. Lodge poles creaked and strained at every heavy gust, and sparks from the fires inside the lodges sped down the wind, to fade and die.

In his lodge War Eagle waited for us, and when we entered he greeted us warmly, but failed to mention the gale. "I have been waiting," he said. "You are late and the story I shall tell you is longer than many of the others." Without further delay the story-telling commenced.

"Once *Old*-man came upon a lodge in the forest. It was a fine one, and painted with strange signs. Smoke was curling from the top, and thus he knew that the person who lived there was at home. Without calling or speaking, he entered the lodge and saw a man sitting by the fire smoking his pipe. The man didn't speak, nor did he offer his pipe to *Old*-man, as our people do when they are glad to see visitors. He didn't even look at his guest, but *Old*-man has no good manners at all. He couldn't see that he wasn't wanted, as he looked about the man's lodge and made himself at home. The linings were beautiful and were painted with fine skill. The lodge was clean and the fire was bright, but there was no woman about.

"Leaning against a fine back-rest, *Old*-man filled his own pipe and lighted it with a coal from the man's fire. Then he began to smoke and look around, wondering why the man acted so queerly. He saw a star that shone down through the smoke-hole, and the tops of several trees that were near the lodge. Then he saw a woman — way up in a tree top and right over the lodge. She looked young and beautiful and tall.

"'Whose woman is that up there in the tree top?' asked *Old*-man.

"'She's your woman if you can catch her

and will marry her,' growled the man; 'but you will have to live here and help me make a living.'

"'I 'll try to catch her, and if I do I will marry her and stay here, for I am a great hunter and can easily kill what meat we want,' said *Old*-man.

"He went out of the lodge and climbed the tree after the woman. She screamed, but he caught her and held her, although she scratched him badly. He carried her into the lodge and there renewed his promise to stay there always. The man married them, and they were happy for four days, but on the fifth morning *Old*-man was gone — gone with all the dried meat in the lodge — the thief.

"When they were sure that the rascal had run away the woman began to cry, but not so the man. He got his bow and arrows and left the lodge in anger. There was snow on the ground and the man took the track of *Old*-man, intending to catch and kill him.

"The track was fresh and the man started on a run, for he was a good hunter and as fast as a Deer. Of course he gained on *Old*-man, who was a much slower traveller; and the Sun was not very high when the old thief stopped on a hilltop to look back. He saw the man coming fast.

"'This will never do,' he said to himself. 'That queer person will catch me. I know what I shall do; I shall turn myself into a dead Bull-Elk and lie down. Then he will pass me and I can go where I please.'

"He took off his moccasins and said to them: 'Moccasins, go on toward the west. Keep going and making plain tracks in the snow toward the big-water where the Sun sleeps. The queer-one will follow you, and when you pass out of the snowy country, you can lose him. Go quickly for he is close upon us.'

"The moccasins ran away as *Old*-man wanted them to, and they made plain tracks in the snow leading away toward the big-water. *Old*-man turned into a dead Bull-Elk and stretched himself near the tracks the moccasins had made.

"Up the hill came the man, his breath short from running. He saw the dead Elk, and thought it might be *Old*-man playing a trick. He was about to shoot an arrow into the dead Elk to make sure; but just as he was about to let the arrow go, he saw the tracks the moccasins had made. Of course he thought the moccasins were on *Old*-man's feet, and that the carcass was really that of a dead Elk. He was badly fooled and took the tracks again. On and on he went, following the moccasins over hills and rivers. Faster than before went the man, and still faster travelled the empty moccasins, the trail growing dimmer and dimmer as the daylight faded. All day long, and all of the night the man followed the tracks without rest or food, and just at daybreak he came to the shore of the big-water.

There, right by the water's edge, stood the empty moccasins, side by side.

"The man turned and looked back. His eyes were red and his legs were trembling. 'Caw — caw, caw,' he heard a Crow say. Right over his head he saw the black bird and knew him, too.

"'Ho! *Old*-man, you were in that dead Bull-Elk. You fooled me, and now you are a Crow. You think you will escape me, do you? Well, you will not; for I, too, know magic, and am wise.'

"With a stick the man drew a cricle in the sand. Then he stood within the ring and sang a song. *Old*-man was worried and watched the strange doings from the air overhead. Inside the circle the man began to whirl about so rapidly that he faded from sight, and from the centre of the circle there came an Eagle. Straight at the Crow flew the Eagle, and away toward the mountains sped the Crow, in fright.

111

"The Crow knew that the Eagle would catch him, so that as soon as he reached the trees on the mountains he turned himself into a Wren and sought the small bushes under the tall trees. The Eagle saw the change, and at once began turning over and over in the air. When he had reached the ground, instead of an Eagle a Sparrow-hawk chased the Wren. Now the chase was fast indeed, for no place could the Wren find in which to hide from the Sparrow-hawk. Through the brush, into trees, among the weeds and grass, flew the Wren with the Hawk close behind. Once the Sparrow-hawk picked a feather from the Wren's tail — so close was he to his victim. It was nearly over with the Wren, when he suddenly came to a park along a river's side. In this park were a hundred lodges of our people, and before a fine lodge there sat the daughter of the chief. It was growing dark and chilly, but still she sat there looking at the river. The Sparrow-hawk was striking at the Wren with his beak and talons, when the Wren saw the young-woman and flew straight to her. So swift he flew that the young-woman didn't see him at all, but she felt something strike her hand, and when she looked she saw a bone ring on her finger. This frightened her, and she ran inside the lodge, where the fire kept the shadows from coming. *Old*-man had changed into the ring, of course, and the Sparrow-hawk didn't dare to go into the lodge; so he stopped outside and listened. This is what he heard *Old*-man say:

"'Don't be frightened, young-woman, I am neither a Wren nor a ring. I am *Old*-man and that Sparrow-hawk has chased me all the day and for nothing. I have never done him harm, and he bothers me without reason.'

"'Liar — forked-tongue,' cried the Sparrow-hawk. 'Believe him not, young-woman. He has done wrong. He is wicked and I am not a Sparrow-hawk, but conscience. Like an arrow I travel, straight and fast. When he lies or steals from his friends I follow him. I talk all the time and he hears me, but lies to himself, and says he does not hear. You know who I am, young-woman, I am what talks inside a person.'

"*Old*-man heard what the Sparrow-hawk said, and he was ashamed for once in his life. He crawled out of the lodge. Into the shadows he ran away — away into the night, and the darkness — away from himself!

"You see," said War Eagle, as he reached for his pipe, "*Old*-man knew that he had done wrong, and his heart troubled him, just as yours will bother you if you do not listen to the voice that speaks within yourselves. Whenever that voice says a thing is wicked, it is wicked — no matter who says it is not. Yes — it is very hard for a man to hide from himself. Ho!"

OLD–MAN'S TREACHERY

OLD–MAN'S TREACHERY

THE next afternoon Muskrat and Fine Bow went hunting. They hid themselves in some brush which grew beside an old game trail that followed the river, and there waited for a chance deer.

Chickadees hopped and called, "chick-a-de-de-de" in the willows and wild-rose bushes that grew near their hiding-place; and the gentle little birds with their pretty coats were often within a few inches of the hands of the young hunters. In perfect silence they watched and admired these little friends, while glance or smile conveyed their appreciation of the bird-visits to each other.

The wind was coming down the stream, and therefore the eyes of the boys seldom left the trail in that direction; for from that quarter an approaching deer would be unwarned by the ever-busy breeze. A rabbit came hopping down the game trail in believed perfect security, passing so close to Fine Bow that he could not resist the desire to strike at him with an arrow. Both boys were obliged to cover their mouths with their open hands to keep from laughing aloud at the surprise and speed shown by the frightened bunny, as he scurried around a bend in the trail, with his white, pudgy tail bobbing rapidly.

They had scarcely regained their composure and silence when, "snap!" went a dry stick. The sharp sound sent a thrill through the hearts of the boys, and instantly they became rigidly watchful. Not a leaf could move on the ground now — not a bush might bend or a bird pass and escape being seen by the four sharp eyes that peered from the brush in the direction indicated by the sound of the breaking stick. Two hearts beat loudly as Fine Bow fitted his arrow to the bowstring. Tense and expectant they waited — yes, it was a deer — a buck, too, and he was coming down the trail, alert and watchful — down the trail that he had often travelled and knew so well. Yes, he had followed his mother along that trail when he was but a spotted fawn — now he wore antlers, and was master of his own ways. On he came — nearly to the brush that hid the hunters, when, throwing his beautiful head high in the air, he stopped, turning his side a trifle.

Zipp — went the arrow and, kicking out behind, away went the buck, crashing through willows and alders that grew in his way, until he was out of sight. Then all was still, save the chick-a-de-de-de, chick-a-de-de-de, that came constantly from the bushes about them.

Out from the cover came the hunters, and with ready bow they followed along the trail. Yes — there was blood on a log, and more on the dead leaves. The arrow had found its mark and they must go slowly in their trailing, lest they lose the meat. For two hours they followed the wounded animal, and at last came upon him in a willow thicket — sick unto death, for the arrow was deep in his paunch. His sufferings were ended by another arrow, and the chase was done.

With their knives the boys dressed the buck, and then went back to the camp to tell the women where the meat could be found — just as the men do. It was their first deer; and pride shone in their faces as they told their grandfather that night in the lodge.

"That is good," War Eagle replied, as the boys finished telling of their success. "That is good, if your mother needed the meat, but it is wrong to kill when you have plenty, lest Manitou be angry. There is always enough, but none to waste, and the hunter who kills more than he needs is wicked. To-night I shall tell you what happened to *Old*-man when he did that. Yes, and he got into trouble over it.

"One day in the fall when the leaves were yellow, and the Deer-people were dressed in their blue robes — when the Geese and Duck-people were travelling to the country where water does not freeze, and where flowers never die, *Old*-man was travelling on the plains.

"Near sundown he saw two Buffalo-Bulls feeding on a steep hillside; but he had no bow and arrow with him. He was hungry, and began to think of some way to kill one of the Bulls for meat. Very soon he thought out a plan, for he is cunning always.

"He ran around the hill out of sight of the Bulls, and there made two men out of grass and sage-brush. They were dummies, of course, but he made them to look just like real men, and then armed each with a wooden knife of great length. Then he set them in the position of fighting; made them look as though they were about to fight each other with the knives. When he had them both fixed to suit, he ran back to the place where the Buffalo were calling:

"'Ho! brothers, wait for me — do not run

away. There are two fine men on the other side of this hill, and they are quarrelling. They will surely fight unless we stop them. It all started over you two Bulls, too. One of the men says you are fat and fine, and the other claims you are poor and skinny. Don't let our brothers fight over such a foolish thing as that. It would be wicked. Now I can decide it, if you will let me feel all over you to see if you are fat or poor. Then I will go back to the men and settle the trouble by telling them the truth. Stand still and let me feel your sides — quick, lest the fight begin while I am away.'

"'All right,' said the Bulls, 'but don't you tickle us.' Then *Old*-man walked up close and commenced to feel about the Bulls' sides; but his heart was bad. From his robe he slipped his great knife, and slyly felt about till he found the spot where the heart beats, and then stabbed the knife into the place, clear up to the hilt.

INDIAN WHY STORIES

"Both of the Bulls died right away, and *Old*-man laughed at the trick he had played upon them. Then he gave a knife to both of his hands, and said:

"'Get to work, both of you! Skin these Bulls while I sit here and boss you.'

"Both hands commenced to skin the Buffalo, but the right hand was much the swifter worker. It gained upon the left hand rapidly, and this made the left hand angry. Finally the left hand called the right hand 'dog-face.' That is the very worst thing you can call a person in our language, you know, and of course it made the right hand angry. So crazy and angry was the right hand that it stabbed the left hand, and then they began to fight in earnest.

"Both cut and slashed till blood covered the animals they were skinning. All this fighting hurt *Old*-man badly, of course, and he commenced to cry, as women do sometimes. This stopped the fight; but still *Old*-man cried,

123

till, drying his tears, he saw a Red Fox sitting near the Bulls, watching him. 'Hi, there, you — go away from there! If you want meat you go and kill it, as I did.'

"Red Fox laughed — 'Ha! — Ha! — Ha! — foolish *Old*-man — Ha! — ha!' Then he ran away and told the other Foxes and the Wolves and the Coyotes about *Old*-man's meat. Told them that his own hands couldn't get along with themselves and that it would be easy to steal it from him.

"They all followed the Red Fox back to the place where *Old*-man was, and there they ate all of the meat — every bit, and polished the bones.

"*Old*-man couldn't stop them, because he was hurt, you see; but it all came about through lying and killing more meat than he needed. Yes — he lied and that is bad, but his hands got to quarrelling between themselves, and family quarrels are always bad. Do not lie; do not quarrel. It is bad. Ho!"

WHY THE NIGHT–HAWK'S WINGS ARE
BEAUTIFUL

WHY THE NIGHT-HAWK'S WINGS ARE
BEAUTIFUL

I WAS awakened by the voice of the camp-
crier, and although it was yet dark I listened
to his message.

The camp was to move. All were to go to
the mouth of the Maria's — "The River That
Scolds at the Other" — the Indians call this
stream, that disturbs the waters of the Missouri with its swifter flood.

On through the camp the crier rode, and
behind him the lodge-fires glowed in answer
to his call. The village was awake, and soon
the thunder of hundreds of hoofs told me that
the pony-bands were being driven into camp,
where the faithful were being roped for the
journey. Fires flickered in the now fading
darkness, and down came the lodges as though

wizard hands had touched them. Before the sun had come to light the world, we were on our way to "The River That Scolds at the Other."

Not a cloud was in the sky, and the wind was still. The sun came and touched the plains and hilltops with the light that makes all wild things glad. Here and there a jack-rabbit scurried away, often followed by a pack of dogs, and sometimes, though not often, they were overtaken and devoured on the spot. Bands of graceful antelope bounded out of our way, stopping on a knoll to watch the strange procession with wondering eyes, and once we saw a dust-cloud raised by a moving herd of buffalo, in the distance.

So the day wore on, the scene constantly changing as we travelled. Wolves and coyotes looked at us from almost every knoll and hill-top; and sage-hens sneaked to cover among the patches of sage-brush, scarcely ten feet away from our ponies. Toward sundown we reached a grove of cottonwoods near the mouth of the Maria's, and in an incredibly short space of time the lodges took form. Soon, from out the tops of a hundred camps, smoke was curling just as though the lodges had been there always, and would forever remain.

As soon as supper was over I found the children, and together we sought War Eagle's lodge. He was in a happy mood and insisted upon smoking two pipes before commencing his story-telling. At last he said:

"To-night I shall tell you why the Night-hawk wears fine clothes. My grandfather told me about it when I was young. I am sure you have seen the Night-hawk sailing over you, dipping and making that strange noise. Of course there is a reason for it.

"*Old*-man was travelling one day in the springtime; but the weather was fine for that time of year. He stopped often and spoke to the bird-people and to the animal-people, for he was in good humor that day. He talked

pleasantly with the trees, and his heart grew
tender. That is, he had good thoughts; and
of course they made him happy. Finally he
felt tired and sat down to rest on a big, round
stone — the kind of stone our white friend
there calls a bowlder. Here he rested for a
while, but the stone was cold, and he felt it
through his robe; so he said:

"'Stone, you seem cold to-day. You may
have my robe. I have hundreds of robes in
my camp, and I don't need this one at all.'
That was a lie he told about having so many
robes. All he had was the one he wore.

"He spread his robe over the stone, and
then started down the hill, naked, for it was
really a fine day. But storms hide in the
mountains, and are never far away when it is
springtime. Soon it began to snow — then
the wind blew from the north with a good
strength behind it. *Old*-man said:

"'Well, I guess I do need that robe myself,
after all. That stone never did anything for

me anyhow. Nobody is ever good to a stone. I 'll just go back and get my robe.'

"Back he went and found the stone. Then he pulled the robe away, and wrapped it about himself. Ho! but that made the stone angry — Ho! *Old*-man started to run down the hill, and the stone ran after him. Ho! it was a funny race they made, over the grass, over smaller stones, and over logs that lay in the way, but *Old*-man managed to keep ahead until he stubbed his toe on a big sage-brush, and fell — swow!

"'Now I have you!' cried the stone — 'now I 'll kill you, too! Now I will teach you to give presents and then take them away,' and the stone rolled right on top of *Old*-man, and sat on his back.

"It was a big stone, you see, and *Old*-man couldn't move it at all. He tried to throw off the stone but failed. He squirmed and twisted — no use — the stone held him fast. He called the stone some names that are not good; but that never helps any. At last he began to call:

"'Help! — Help! — Help!' but nobody heard him except the Night-hawk, and he told the *Old*-man that he would help him all he could; so he flew away up in the air — so far that he looked like a black speck. Then he came down straight and struck that rock an awful blow — 'swow!' — and broke it in two pieces. Indeed he did. The blow was so great that it spoiled the Night-hawk's bill, forever — made it queer in shape, and jammed his head, so that it is queer, too. But he broke the rock, and *Old*-man stood upon his feet.

"'Thank you, Brother Night-hawk,' said *Old*-man, 'now I will do something for you. I am going to make you different from other birds — make you so people will always notice you.'

"You know that when you break a rock the powdered stone is white, like snow; and there is always some of the white powder whenever you break a rock, by pounding it. Well, *Old*-man took some of the fine powdered stone and shook it on the Night-hawk's wings in spots and stripes — made the great white stripes you have seen on his wings, and told him that no other bird could have such marks on his clothes.

"All the Night-hawk's children dress the same way now; and they always will as long as there are Night-hawks. Of course their clothes make them proud; and that is why they keep at flying over people's heads — soaring and dipping and turning all the time, to show off their pretty wings.

"That is all for to-night. Muskrat, tell your father I would run Buffalo with him to-morrow — Ho!"

WHY THE MOUNTAIN-LION IS
LONG AND LEAN

WHY THE MOUNTAIN–LION IS
LONG AND LEAN

HAVE you ever seen the plains in the morning — a June morning, when the spurred lark soars and sings — when the plover calls, and the curlew pipes his shriller notes to the rising sun? Then is there music, indeed, for no bird outsings the spurred lark; and thanks to *Old*-man he is not wanting in numbers, either. The plains are wonderful then — more wonderful than they are at this season of the year; but at all times they beckon and hold one as in a spell, especially when they are backed or bordered by a snow-capped mountain range. Looking toward the east they are boundless, but on their western edge superb mountains rear themselves.

All over this vast country the Indians roamed, following the great buffalo herds as

137

did the wolves, and making their living with the bow and lance, since the horse came to them. In the very old days the "piskun" was used, and buffalo were enticed to follow a fantastically dressed man toward a cliff, far enough to get the herd moving in that direction, when the "buffalo-man" gained cover, and hidden Indians raised from their hiding-places behind the animals, and drove them over the cliff, where they were killed in large numbers.

Not until Cortez came with his cavalry from Spain, were there horses on this continent, and then generations passed ere the plains tribes possessed this valuable animal, that so materially changed their lives. Dogs dragged the Indian's travois or packed his household goods in the days before the horse came, and for hundreds — perhaps thousands of years, these people had no other means of transporting their goods and chattels. As the Indian is slow to forget or change the ways of his father, we should pause before we brand him as wholly improvident, I think.

He has always been a family-man, has the Indian, and small children had to be carried, as well as his camp equipage. Wolf-dogs had to be fed, too, in some way, thus adding to his burden; for it took a great many to make it possible for him to travel at all.

When the night came and we visited War Eagle, we found he had other company — so we waited until their visit was ended before settling ourselves to hear the story that he might tell us.

"The Crows have stolen some of our best horses," said War Eagle, as soon as the other guests had gone. "That is all right — we shall get them back, and more, too. The Crows have only borrowed those horses and will pay for their use with others of their own. To-night I shall tell you why the Mountain-lion is so long and thin and why he wears hair that looks singed. I shall also tell you

139

why that person's nose is black, because it is part of the story.

"A long time ago the Mountain-lion was a short, thick-set person. I am sure you didn't guess that. He was always a great thief like *Old*-man, but once he went too far, as you shall see.

"One day *Old*-man was on a hilltop, and saw smoke curling up through the trees, away off on the far side of a gulch. 'Ho!' he said, 'I wonder who builds fires except me. I guess I will go and find out.'

"He crossed the gulch and crept carefully toward the smoke. When he got quite near where the fire was, he stopped and listened. He heard some loud laughing but could not see who it was that felt so glad and gay. Finally he crawled closer and peeked through the brush toward the fire. Then he saw some Squirrel-people, and they were playing some sort of game. They were running and laughing, and having a big time, too. What do you think they were doing? They were running about the fire — all chasing one Squirrel. As soon as the Squirrel was caught, they would bury him in the ashes near the fire until he cried; then they would dig him out in a hurry. Then another Squirrel would take the lead and run until he was caught, as the other had been. In turn the captive would submit to being buried, and so on — while the racing and laughing continued. They never left the buried one in the ashes after he cried, but always kept their promise and dug him out, right away.

"'Say, let me play, won't you?' asked *Old*-man. But the Squirrel-people all ran away, and he had a hard time getting them to return to the fire.

"'You can't play this game,' replied the Chief-Squirrel, after they had returned to the fire.

"'Yes, I can,' declared *Old*-man, 'and you may bury me first, but be sure to dig me out when I cry, and not let me burn, for those ashes are hot near the fire.'

"'All right,' said the Chief-Squirrel, 'we will let you play. Lie down,' — and *Old*-man did lie down near the fire. Then the Squirrels began to laugh and bury *Old*-man in the ashes, as they did their own kind. In no time at all *Old*-man cried: 'Ouch! — you are burning me — quick! — dig me out.'

"True to their promise, the Squirrel-people dug *Old*-man out of the ashes, and laughed at him because he cried so quickly.

"'Now, it is my turn to cover the captive,' said *Old*-man, 'and as there are so many of you, I have a scheme that will make the game funnier and shorter. All of you lie down at once in a row. Then I will cover you all at one time. When you cry — I will dig you out right away and the game will be over.'

"They didn't know *Old*-man very well; so they said, 'all right,' and then they all laid down in a row about the fire.

"*Old*-man buried them all in the ashes — then he threw some more wood on the fire and went away and left them. Every Squirrel there was in the world was buried in the ashes except one woman Squirrel, and she told *Old*-man she couldn't play and had to go home. If she hadn't gone, there might not be any Squirrels in this world right now. Yes, it is lucky that she went home.

"For a minute or so *Old*-man watched the fire as it grew hotter, and then went down to a creek where willows grew and made himself a great plate by weaving them together. When he had finished making the plate, he returned to the fire, and it had burned low again. He laughed at his wicked work, and a Raven, flying over just then, called him 'forked-tongue,' or liar, but he didn't mind that at all. *Old*-man cut a long stick and began to dig out the Squirrel-people. One by one he fished them out of the hot ashes; and they were roasted fine and were ready to eat. As he fished them out he counted them, and laid them on the willow plate he had made. When he had dug out the last one, he took the plate to the creek and there sat down to eat the Squirrels, for he was hungry, as usual. *Old*-man is a big eater, but he couldn't eat all of the Squirrels at once, and while eating he fell asleep with the great plate in his lap.

"Nobody knows how long it was that he slept, but when he waked his plate of Squirrels was gone — gone completely. He looked behind him; he looked about him; but the plate was surely gone. Ho! But he was angry. He stamped about in the brush and called aloud to those who might hear him; but nobody answered, and then he started to look for the thief. *Old*-man has sharp eyes, and he found the trail in the grass where somebody had passed while he slept. 'Ho!' he said, 'the Mountain-lion has stolen my Squirrels. I see his footprints; see where he has mashed

144

the grass as he walked with those soft feet of his; but I shall find him, for I made him and know all his ways.'

"*Old*-man got down on his hands and knees to walk as the Bear-people do, just as he did that night in the Sun's lodge, and followed the trail of the Mountain-lion over the hills and through the swamps. At last he came to a place where the grass was all bent down, and there he found his willow plate, but it was empty. That was the place where the Mountain-lion had stopped to eat the rest of the Squirrels, you know; but he didn't stay there long because he expected that *Old*-man would try to follow him.

"The Mountain-lion had eaten so much that he was sleepy and, after travelling a while after he had eaten the Squirrels, he thought he would rest. He hadn't intended to go to sleep; but he crawled upon a big stone near the foot of a hill and sat down where he could see a long way. Here his eyes began to wink, and his head began to nod, and finally he slept.

"Without stopping once, *Old*-man kept on the trail. That is what counts — sticking right to the thing you are doing — and just before sundown *Old*-man saw the sleeping Lion. Carefully, lest he wake the sleeper, *Old*-man crept close, being particular not to move a stone or break a twig; for the Mountain-lion is much faster than men are, you see; and if *Old*-man had wakened the Lion, he would never have caught him again, perhaps. Little by little he crept to the stone where the Mountain-lion was dreaming, and at last grabbed him by the tail. It wasn't much of a tail then, but enough for *Old*-man to hold to. Ho! The Lion was scared and begged hard, saying:

"'Spare me, *Old*-man. You were full and I was hungry. I had to have something to eat; had to get my living. Please let me go and do not hurt me.' Ho! *Old*-man was angry — more angry than he was when he

146

waked and found that he had been robbed, because he had travelled so far on his hands and knees.

"'I'll show you. I'll teach you. I'll fix you, right now. Steal from me, will you? Steal from the man that made you, you night-prowling rascal!'

"*Old*-man put his foot behind the Mountain-lion's head, and, still holding the tail, pulled hard and long, stretching the Lion out to great length. He squalled and cried, but *Old*-man kept pulling until he nearly broke the Mountain-lion in two pieces — until he couldn't stretch him any more. Then *Old*-man put his foot on the Mountain-lion's back, and, still holding the tail, stretched that out until the tail was nearly as long as the body.

"'There, you thief — now you are too long and lean to get fat, and you shall always look just like that. Your children shall all grow to look the same way, just to pay you for your

147

stealing from the man that made you. Come on with me'; and he dragged the poor Lion back to the place where the fire was, and there rolled him in the hot ashes, singeing his robe till it looked a great deal like burnt hair. Then *Old*-man stuck the Lion's nose against the burnt logs and blackened it some — that is why his face looks as it does to-day.

"The Mountain-lion was lame and sore, but *Old*-man scolded him some more and told him that it would take lots more food to keep him after that, and that he would have to work harder to get his living, to pay for what he had done. Then he said, 'go now, and remember all the Mountain-lions that ever live shall look just as you do.' And they do, too!

"That is the story — that is why the Mountain-lion is so long and lean, but he is no bigger thief than *Old*-man, nor does he tell any more lies. Ho!"

THE FIRE–LEGGINGS

THE FIRE–LEGGINGS

THERE had been a sudden change in the weather. A cold rain was falling, and the night comes early when the clouds hang low. The children loved a bright fire, and to-night War Eagle's lodge was light as day. Away off on the plains a wolf was howling, and the rain pattered upon the lodge as though it never intended to quit. It was a splendid night for story-telling, and War Eagle filled and lighted the great stone pipe, while the children made themselves comfortable about the fire.

A spark sprang from the burning sticks, and fell upon Fine Bow's bare leg. They all laughed heartily at the boy's antics to rid himself of the burning coal; and as soon as the laughing ceased War Eagle laid aside the pipe. An Indian's pipe is large to look at, but holds little tobacco.

"See your shadows on the lodge wall?" asked the old warrior. The children said they saw them, and he continued:

"Some day I will tell you a story about them, and how they drew the arrows of our enemies, but to-night I am going to tell you of the great fire-leggings.

"It was long before there were men and women on the world, but my grandfather told me what I shall now tell you.

"The gray light that hides the night-stars was creeping through the forests, and the wind the Sun sends to warn the people of his coming was among the fir tops. Flowers, on slender stems, bent their heads out of respect for the herald-wind's Master, and from the dead top of a pine-tree the Yellowhammer beat upon his drum and called 'the Sun is awake — all hail the Sun!'

"Then the bush-birds began to sing the song of the morning, and from alders the Robins joined, until all live things were awakened by

152

the great music. Where the tall ferns grew, the Doe waked her Fawns, and taught them to do homage to the Great Light. In the creeks, where the water was still and clear, and where throughout the day, like a delicate damaskeen, the shadows of leaves that over-hang would lie, the Speckled Trout broke the surface of the pool in his gladness of the com-ing day. Pine-squirrels chattered gayly, and loudly proclaimed what the wind had told; and all the shadows were preparing for a great journey to the Sand Hills, where the ghost-people dwell.

"Under a great spruce-tree — where the ground was soft and dry, *Old*-man slept. The joy that thrilled creation disturbed him not, although the Sun was near. The bird-people looked at the sleeper in wonder, but the Pine-squirrel climbed the great spruce-tree with a pine-cone in his mouth. Quickly he ran out on the limb that spread over *Old*-man, and dropped the cone on the sleeper's face. Then he scolded *Old*-man, saying: 'Get up — get up — lazy one — lazy one — get up — get up.'

"Rubbing his eyes in anger, *Old*-man sat up and saw the Sun coming — his hunting leggings slipping through the thickets — setting them afire, till all the Deer and Elk ran out and sought new places to hide.

"'Ho, Sun!' called *Old*-man, 'those are mighty leggings you wear. No wonder you are a great hunter. Your leggings set fire to all the thickets, and by the light you can easily see the Deer and Elk; they cannot hide. Ho! Give them to me and I shall then be the great hunter and never be hungry.'

"'Good,' said the Sun, 'take them, and let me see you wear my leggings.'

"*Old*-man was glad in his heart, for he was lazy, and now he thought he could kill the game without much work, and that he could be a great hunter — as great as the Sun. He put on the leggings and at once began to hunt the thickets, for he was hungry. Very soon

the leggings began to burn his legs. The faster
he travelled the hotter they grew, until in pain
he cried out to the Sun to come and take back
his leggings; but the Sun would not hear him.
On and on *Old*-man ran. Faster and faster he
flew through the country, setting fire to the
brush and grass as he passed. Finally he came
to a great river, and jumped in. Sizzzzzzz —
the water said, when *Old*-man's legs touched it.
It cried out, as it does when it is sprinkled upon
hot stones in the sweat-lodge, for the leggings
were very hot. But standing in the cool water
Old-man took off the leggings and threw them
out upon the shore, where the Sun found them
later in the day.

"The Sun's clothes were too big for *Old*-
man, and his work too great.

"We should never ask to do the things which
Manitou did not intend us to do. If we keep
this always in mind we shall never get into
trouble.

"Be yourselves always. That is what Manitou intended.   Never blame the Wolf for what he does. He was made to do such things. Now I want you to go to your fathers' lodges and sleep. To-morrow night I will tell you why there are so many snakes in the world. Ho!"

THE MOON AND THE GREAT SNAKE

THE MOON AND THE GREAT SNAKE

THE rain had passed; the moon looked down from a clear sky, and the bushes and dead grass smelled wet, after the heavy storm. A cottontail ran into a clump of wild-rose bushes near War Eagle's lodge, and some dogs were close behind the frightened animal, as he gained cover. Little Buffalo Calf threw a stone into the bushes, scaring the rabbit from his hiding-place, and away went bunny, followed by the yelping pack. We stood and listened until the noise of the chase died away, and then went into the lodge, where we were greeted, as usual, by War Eagle. To-night he smoked; but with greater ceremony, and I suspected that it had something to do with the forthcoming story. Finally he said:

"You have seen many Snakes, I suppose?"

"Yes," replied the children, "we have seen a great many. In the summer we see them every day."

"Well," continued the story-teller, "once there was only one Snake on the whole world, and he was a big one, I tell you. He was pretty to look at, and was painted with all the colors we know. This snake was proud of his clothes and· had a wicked heart. Most Snakes are wicked, because they are his relations.

"Now, I have not told you all about it yet, nor will I tell you to-night, but the Moon is the Sun's wife, and some day I shall tell you that story, but to-night I am telling you about the Snakes.

"You know that the Sun goes early to bed, and that the Moon most always leaves before he gets to the lodge. Sometimes this is not so, but that is part of another story.

"This big Snake used to crawl up a high hill and watch the Moon in the sky. He was in love with her, and she knew. it; but she paid

160

no attention to him. She liked his looks, for his clothes were fine, and he was always slick and smooth. This went on for a long time, but she never talked to him at all. The Snake thought maybe the hill wasn't high enough, so he found a higher one, and watched the Moon pass, from the top. Every night he climbed this high hill and motioned to her. She began to pay more attention to the big Snake, and one morning early, she loafed at her work a little, and spoke to him. He was flattered, and so was she, because he said many nice things to her, but she went on to the Sun's lodge, and left the Snake.

"The next morning very early she saw the Snake again, and this time she stopped a long time — so long that the Sun had started out from the lodge before she reached home. He wondered what kept her so long, and became suspicious of the Snake. He made up his mind to watch, and try to catch them together. So every morning the Sun left the lodge a little earlier than before; and one morning, just as he climbed a mountain, he saw the big Snake talking to the Moon. That made him angry, and you can't blame him, because his wife was spending her time loafing with a Snake.

"She ran away; ran to the Sun's lodge and left the Snake on the hill. In no time the Sun had grabbed him. My, the Sun was angry! The big Snake begged, and promised never to speak to the Moon again, but the Sun had him; and he smashed him into thousands of little pieces, all of different colors from the different parts of his painted body. The little pieces each turned into a little snake, just as you see them now, but they were all too small for the Moon to notice after that. That is how so many Snakes came into the world; and that is why they are all small, nowadays.

"Our people do not like the Snake-people very well, but we know that they were made to do something on this world, and that they do it, or they wouldn't live here.

"That was a short story, but to-morrow night I will tell you why the Deer-people have no gall on their livers; and why the Antelope-people do not wear dew-claws, for you should know that there are no other animals with cloven hoofs that are like them in this.

"I am tired to-night, and I will ask that you go to your lodges, that I may sleep, for I am getting old.   Ho!"

WHY THE DEER HAS NO GALL

WHY THE DEER HAS NO GALL

BRIGHT and early the next morning the children were playing on the bank of "The River That Scolds the Other," when Fine Bow said:

"Let us find a Deer's foot, and the foot of an Antelope and look at them, for to-night grandfather will tell us why the Deer has the dew-claws, and why the Antelope has none."

"Yes, and let us ask mother if the Deer has no gall on its liver. Maybe she can show both the liver of a Deer and that of an Antelope; then we can see for ourselves," said Blue-bird.

So they began to look about where the hides had been grained for tanning; and sure enough, there were the feet of both the antelope and the deer. On the deer's feet, or legs, they found the dew-claws, but on the antelope there were none. This made them all anxious to know why these animals, so nearly alike, should differ in this way.

Bluebird's mother passed the children on her way to the river for water, and the little girl asked: "Say, mother, does the Deer have gall on his liver?"

"No, my child, but the Antelope does; and your grandfather will tell you why if you ask him."

That night in the lodge War Eagle placed before his grandchildren the leg of a deer and the leg of an antelope, as well as the liver of a deer and the liver of an antelope.

"See for yourselves that this thing is true, before I tell you why it is so, and how it happened."

"We see," they replied, "and to-day we found that these strange things are true, but we don't know why, grandfather."

"Of course you don't know why. Nobody

knows that until he is told, and now I shall tell you, so you will always know, and tell your children, that they, too, may know.

"It was long, long ago, of course. All these things happened long ago when the world was young, as you are now. It was on a summer morning, and the Deer was travelling across the plains country to reach the mountains on the far-off side, where he had relatives. He grew thirsty, for it was very warm, and stopped to drink from a water-hole on the plains. When he had finished drinking he looked up, and there was his own cousin, the Antelope, drinking near him.

"'Good morning, cousin,' said the Deer. 'It is a warm morning and water tastes good, doesn't it?'

"'Yes,' replied the Antelope, 'it is warm to-day, but I can beat you running, just the same.'

"'Ha-ha!' laughed the Deer — 'you beat me running? Why, you can't run half as fast as

I can, but if you want to run a race let us bet
something. What shall it be?'

"'I will bet you my gall-sack,' replied the
Antelope.

"'Good,' said the Deer, 'but let us run toward that range of mountains, for I am going
that way, anyhow, to see my relations.'

"'All right,' said the Antelope. 'All ready,
and here we go.'

"Away they ran toward the far-off range.
All the way the Antelope was far ahead of the
Deer; and just at the foot of the mountains
he stopped to wait for him to catch up.

"Both were out of breath from running, but
both declared they had done their best, and the
Deer, being beaten, gave the Antelope his sack
of gall.

"'This ground is too flat for me,' said the
Deer. 'Come up the hillside where the gulches
cut the country, and rocks are in our way,
and I will show you how to run. I can't run
on flat ground. It's too easy for me.'

"'All right,' replied the Antelope, 'I will run another race with you on your own ground, and I think I can beat you there, too.'

"Together they climbed the hill until they reached a rough country, when the Deer said:

"'This is my kind of country. Let us run a race here. Whoever gets ahead and stays there, must keep on running until the other calls on him to stop.'

"'That suits me,' replied the Antelope, 'but what shall we bet this time? I don't want to waste my breath for nothing. I'll tell you — let us bet our dew-claws.'

"'Good. I'll bet you my dew-claws against your own, that I can beat you again. Are you all ready? — Go!'

"Away they went over logs, over stones and across great gulches that cut the hills in two. On and on they ran, with the Deer far ahead of the Antelope. Both were getting tired, when the Antelope called:

"'Hi, there — you! Stop, you can beat me. I give up.'

"So the Deer stopped and waited until the Antelope came up to him, and they both laughed over the fun, but the Antelope had to give the Deer his dew-claws, and now he goes without himself. The Deer wears dew-claws and always will, because of that race, but on his liver there is no gall, while the Antelope carries a gall-sack like the other animals with cloven hoofs.

"That is all of that story, but it is too late to tell you another to-night. If you will come to-morrow evening, I will tell you of some trouble that *Old*-man got into once. He deserved it, for he was wicked, as you shall see. Ho!"

WHY THE INDIANS WHIP THE
BUFFALO–BERRIES FROM
THE BUSHES

WHY THE INDIANS WHIP THE BUFFALO–BERRIES FROM THE BUSHES

THE Indian believes that all things live again; that all were created by one and the same power; that nothing was created in vain; and that in the life beyond the grave he will know all things that he knew here. In that other world he expects to make his living easier, and not suffer from hunger or cold; therefore, all things that die must go to his heaven, in order that he may be supplied with the necessities of life.

The sun is not the Indian's God, but a personification of the Deity; His greatest manifestation; His light.

The Indian believes that to each of His creations God gave some peculiar power, and that

the possessors of these special favors are His
lieutenants and keepers of the several special
attributes; such as wisdom, cunning, speed,
and the knowledge of healing wounds. These
wonderful gifts, he knew, were bestowed as
favors by a common God, and therefore he revered these powers, and, without jealousy, paid
tribute thereto.

The bear was great in war, because before
the horse came, he would sometimes charge the
camps and kill or wound many people. Although many arrows were sent into his huge
carcass, he seldom died. Hence the Indian was
sure that the bear could heal his wounds.
That the bear possessed a great knowledge of
roots and berries, the Indian knew, for he often
saw him digging the one and stripping the others from the bushes. The buffalo, the beaver,
the wolf, and the eagle — each possessed strange
powers that commanded the Indian's admira-
tion and respect, as did many other things in
creation.

INDIAN WHY STORIES

If about to go to war, the Indian did not ask his God for aid — oh, no. He realized that God made his enemy, too; and that if He desired that enemy's destruction, it would be accomplished without man's aid. So the Indian sang his song to the bear, prayed to the bear, and thus invoked aid from a brute, and not his God, when he sought to destroy his fellows.

Whenever the Indian addressed the Great God, his prayer was for life, and life alone. He is the most religious man I have ever known, as well as the most superstitious; and there are stories dealing with his religious faith that are startling, indeed.

"It is the wrong time of year to talk about berries," said War Eagle, that night in the lodge, "but I shall tell you why your mothers whip the buffalo-berries from the bushes. *Old*-man was the one who started it, and our people have followed his example ever since. Ho! *Old*-man made a fool of himself that day.

"It was the time when buffalo-berries are

177

red and ripe. All of the bushes along the rivers were loaded with them, and our people were about to gather what they needed, when *Old*-man changed things, as far as the gathering was concerned.

"He was travelling along a river, and hungry, as he always was. Standing on the bank of that river, he saw great clusters of red, ripe buffalo-berries in the water. They were larger than any berries he had ever seen, and he said:

"'I guess I will get those berries. They look fine, and I need them. Besides, some of the people will see them and get them, if I don't.'

"He jumped into the water; looked for the berries; but they were not there. For a time *Old*-man stood in the river and looked for the berries, but they were gone.

"After a while he climbed out on the bank again, and when the water got smooth once more there were the berries — the same berries, in the same spot in the water.

"'Ho!—that is a funny thing. I wonder where they hid that time. I must have those berries!' he said to himself.

"In he went again — splashing the water like a Grizzly Bear. He looked about him and the berries were gone again. The water was rippling about him, but there were no berries at all. He felt on the bottom of the river but they were not there.

"'Well,' he said, 'I will climb out and watch to see where they come from; then I shall grab them when I hit the water next time.'

"He did that; but he couldn't tell where the berries came from. As soon as the water settled and became smooth — there were the berries — the same as before. Ho! — *Old*-man was wild; he was angry, I tell you. And in he went flat on his stomach! He made an awful splash and mussed the water greatly; but there were no berries.

"'I know what I shall do. I will stay right

here and wait for those berries; that is what I shall do'; and he did.

"He thought maybe somebody was looking at him and would laugh, so he glanced along the bank. And there, right over the water, he saw the same bunch of berries on some tall bushes. Don't you see? *Old*-man saw the shadow of the berry-bunch; not the berries. He saw the red shadow-berries on the water; that was all, and he was such a fool he didn't know they were not real.

"Well, now he was angry in truth. Now he was ready for war. He climbed out on the bank again and cut a club. Then he went at the buffalo-berry bushes and pounded them till all of the red berries fell upon the ground — till the branches were bare of berries.

"'There,' he said, 'that's what you get for making a fool of the man who made you. You shall be beaten every year as long as you live, to pay for what you have done; you and your children, too.'

"That is how it all came about, and that is why your mothers whip the buffalo-berry bushes and then pick the berries from the ground. Ho!"

OLD–MAN AND THE FOX

OLD-MAN AND THE FOX

I AM sure that the plains Indian never made nor used the stone arrow-head. I have heard white men say that they had seen Indians use them; but I have never found an Indian that ever used them himself, or knew of their having been used by his people. Thirty years ago I knew Indians, intimately, who were nearly a hundred years old, who told me that the stone arrow-head had never been in use in their day, nor had their fathers used them in their own time. Indians find these arrow-points just as they find the stone mauls and hammers, which I have seen them use thousands of times, but they do not make them any more than they make the stone mauls and hammers. In the old days, both the head of the lance and the point of the arrow were of bone; even knives were of bone, but some other people surely made the arrow-points that are scattered throughout the United States and Europe, I am told.

One night I asked War Eagle if he had ever known the use, by Indians, of the stone arrow-head, and he said he had not. He told me that just across the Canadian line there was a small lake, surrounded by trees, wherein there was an island covered with long reeds and grass. All about the edge of this island were willows that grew nearly to the water, but intervening there was a narrow beach of stones. Here, he said, the stone arrow-heads had been made by little ghost-people who lived there, and he assured me that he had often seen these strange little beings when he was a small boy. Whenever his people were camped by this lake the old folks waked the children at daybreak to see the inhabitants of this strange island; and always when a noise was made, or the sun came up, the little people hid away. Often he had seen their heads above the grass and tiny willows, and his grandfather had told him that all the stone arrow-heads had been made on that island, and in war had been shot all over the world, by magic bows.

"No," he said, "I shall not lie to you, my friend. I never saw those little people shoot an arrow, but there are so many arrows there, and so many pieces of broken ones, that it proves that my grandfather was right in what he told me. Besides, nobody could ever sleep on that island."

I have heard a legend wherein *Old*-man, in the beginning, killed an animal for the people to eat, and then instructed them to use the ribs of the dead brute to make knives and arrow-points. I have seen lance-heads, made from shank bones, that were so highly polished that they resembled pearl, and I have in my possession bone arrow-points such as were used long ago. Indians do not readily forget their tribal history, and I have photographed a war-bonnet, made of twisted buffalo hair, that was manufactured before the present owner's people had, or ever saw, the horse. The owner of this bonnet has told me that the stone arrow-head was never used by Indians, and that he knew that ghost-people made and used them when the world was young.

The bow of the plains Indian was from thirty-six to forty-four inches long, and made from the wood of the choke-cherry tree. Sometimes bows were made from the service (or sarvice) berry bush, and this bush furnished the best material for arrows. I have seen hickory bows among the plains Indians, too, and these were longer and always straight, instead of being fashioned like Cupid's weapon. These hickory bows came from the East, of course, and through trading, reached the plains country. I have also seen bows covered with the skins of the bull-snake, or wound with sinew, and bows have been made from the horns of the elk, in the early days, after a long course of preparation.

Before Lewis and Clark crossed this vast country, the Blackfeet had traded with the Hudson Bay Company, and steel knives and lance-heads, bearing the names of English makers, still remain to testify to the relations existing, in those days, between those famous traders and men of the Piegan, Blood, and Blackfoot tribes, although it took many years for traders on our own side of the line to gain their friendship. Indeed, trappers and traders blamed the Hudson Bay Company for the feeling of hatred held by the three tribes of Blackfeet for the "Americans"; and there is no doubt that they were right to some extent, although the killing of the Blackfoot warrior by Captain Lewis in 1805 may have been largely to blame for the trouble. Certain it is that for many years after the killing, the Blackfeet kept traders and trappers on the dodge unless they were Hudson Bay men, and in 1810 drove the "American" trappers and traders from their fort at Three-Forks.

It was early when we gathered in War Eagle's lodge, the children and I, but the story-telling began at once.

"Now I shall tell you a story that will show you how little *Old*-man cared for the welfare of others," said War Eagle.

"It happened in the fall, this thing I shall tell you, and the day was warm and bright. *Old*-man and his brother the Red Fox were travelling together for company. They were on a hillside when *Old*-Man said: 'I am hungry. Can you not kill a Rabbit or something for us to eat? The way is long, and I am getting old, you know. You are swift of foot and cunning, and there are Rabbits among these rocks.'

"'Ever since morning came I have watched for food, but the moon must be wrong or something, for I see nothing that is good to eat,' replied the Fox. 'Besides that, my medicine is bad and my heart is weak. You are great, and I have heard you can do most anything. Many

190

snows have known your footprints, and the snows make us all wise. I think you are the one to help, not I.'

"'Listen, brother,' said *Old*-man, 'I have neither bow nor lance — nothing to use in hunting. Your weapons are ever with you — your great nose and your sharp teeth. Just as we came up this hill I saw two great Buffalo-Bulls. You were not looking, but I saw them, and if you will do as I want you to we shall have plenty of meat. This is my scheme; I shall pull out all of your hair, leaving your body white and smooth, like that of the fish. I shall leave only the white hair that grows on the tip of your tail, and that will make you funny to look at. Then you are to go before the Bulls and commence to dance and act foolish. Of course the Bulls will laugh at you, and as soon as they get to laughing you must act sillier than ever. That will make them laugh so hard that they will fall down and laugh on the ground. When they fall, I shall come upon them with my knife and kill them. Will you do as I suggest, brother, or will you starve?'

"'What! Pull out my hair? I shall freeze with no hair on my body, *Old*-man. No — I will not suffer you to pull my hair out when the winter is so near,' cried the Fox.

"'Ho! It is vanity, my brother, not fear of freezing. If you will do this we shall have meat for the winter, and a fire to keep us warm. See, the wind is in the south and warm. There is no danger of freezing. Come, let me do it,' replied *Old*-man.

"'Well — if you are sure that I won't freeze, all right,' said the Fox, 'but I'll bet I'll be sorry.'

"So *Old*-man pulled out all of the Fox's hair, leaving only the white tip that grew near the end of his tail. Poor little Red Fox shivered in the warm breeze that *Old*-man told about, and kept telling *Old*-man that the hair-pulling hurt badly. Finally *Old*-man finished the job and laughed at the Fox, saying: 'Why, you make me laugh, too. Now go and dance before the Bulls, and I shall watch and be ready for my part of the scheme.'

"Around the hill went the poor Red Fox and found the Bulls. Then he began to dance before them as *Old*-man had told him. The Bulls took one look at the hairless Fox and began to laugh. My! How they did laugh, and then the Red Fox stood upon his hind legs and danced some more; acted sillier, as *Old*-man had told him. Louder and louder laughed the Bulls, until they fell to the ground with their breath short from the laughing. The Red Fox kept at his antics lest the Bulls get up before *Old*-man reached them; but soon he saw him coming, with a knife in his hand.

"Running up to the Bulls, *Old*-man plunged his knife into their hearts, and they died. Into the ground ran their blood, and then *Old*-man laughed and said: 'Ho, I am the smart one. I am the real hunter. I depend on my head for meat — ha! — ha! — ha!'

"Then *Old*-man began to dress and skin the Bulls, and he worked hard and long. In fact it was nearly night when he got the work all done.

"Poor little Red Fox had stood there all the time, and *Old*-man never noticed that the wind had changed and was coming from the north. Yes, poor Red Fox stood there and spoke no word; said nothing at all, even when *Old*-man had finished.

"'Hi, there, you! what's the matter with you? Are you sorry that we have meat? Say, answer me!'

"But the Red Fox was frozen stiff — was dead. Yes, the north wind had killed him while *Old*-man worked at the skinning. The Fox had been caught by the north wind naked, and was dead. *Old*-man built a fire and warmed his hands; that was all he cared for the Red Fox, and that is all he cared for anybody. He might have known that no person could stand the north wind without a robe; but as long as he was warm himself — that was all he wanted.

"That is all of that story. To-morrow night I shall tell you why the birch-tree wears those slashes in its bark. That was some of *Old*-man's work, too. Ho!"

WHY THE BIRCH–TREE WEARS
THE SLASHES IN ITS BARK

WHY THE BIRCH–TREE WEARS
THE SLASHES IN ITS BARK

THE white man has never understood the Indian, and the example set the Western tribes of the plains by our white brethren has not been such as to inspire the red man with either confidence or respect for our laws or our religion. The fighting trapper, the border bandit, the horse-thief and rustler, in whose stomach legitimately acquired beef would cause colic — were the Indians' first acquaintances who wore a white skin, and he did not know that they were not of the best type. Being outlaws in every sense, these men sought shelter from the Indian in the wilderness; and he learned of their ways about his lodge-fire, or in battle, often provoked by the white ruffian in the hope of gain. They lied to the Indian — these first white acquaintances, and in after-years, the great Government of the United States lied and lied again, until he has come to believe that there is no truth in the white man's heart. And I don't blame him.

The Indian is a charitable man. I don't believe he ever refused food and shelter or abused a visitor. He has never been a bigot, and concedes to every other man the right to his own beliefs. Further than that, the Indian believes that every man's religion and belief is right and proper for that man's self.

It was blowing a gale and snow was being driven in fine flakes across the plains when we went to the lodge for a story. Every minute the weather was growing colder, and an early fall storm of severity was upon us. The wind seemed to add to the good nature of our host as he filled and passed me the pipe.

"This is the night I was to tell you about the Birch-Tree, and the wind will help to make you understand," said War Eagle after we had finished smoking.

"Of course," he continued, "this all happened in the summer-time when the weather was warm, very warm. Sometimes, you know, there are great winds in the summer, too.

"It was a hot day, and *Old*-man was trying to sleep, but the heat made him sick. He wandered to a hilltop for air; but there was no air. Then he went down to the river and found no relief. He travelled to the timber-lands, and there the heat was great, although he found plenty of shade. The travelling made him warmer, of course, but he wouldn't stay still.

"By and by he called to the winds to blow, and they commenced. First they didn't blow very hard, because they were afraid they might make *Old*-man angry, but he kept crying:

"'Blow harder — harder — harder! Blow worse than ever you blew before, and send this heat away from the world.'

"So, of course, the winds did blow harder — harder than they ever had blown before.

201

"'Bend and break, Fir-Tree!' cried *Old*-man, and the Fir-Tree did bend and break. 'Bend and break, Pine-Tree!' and the Pine-Tree did bend and break. 'Bend and break, Spruce-Tree!' and the Spruce-Tree did bend and break. 'Bend and break, O Birch-Tree!' and the Birch-Tree did bend, but it wouldn't break — no, sir! — it wouldn't break!

"'Ho! Birch-Tree, won't you mind me? Bend and break! I tell you,' but all the Birch-Tree would do was to bend.

"It bent to the ground; it bent double to please *Old*-man, but it would not break.

"'Blow harder, wind!' cried *Old*-man, 'blow harder and break the Birch-Tree.' The wind tried to blow harder, but it couldn't, and that made the thing worse, because *Old*-man was so angry he went crazy. 'Break! I tell you — break!' screamed *Old*-man to the Birch-Tree.

"'I won't break,' replied the Birch; 'I shall never break for any wind. I will bend, but I shall never, never break.'

"'You won't, hey?' cried *Old*-man, and he rushed at the Birch-Tree with his hunting-knife. He grabbed the top of the Birch because it was touching the ground, and began slashing the bark of the Birch-Tree with the knife. All up and down the trunk of the tree *Old*-man slashed, until the Birch was covered with the knife slashes.

"'There! that is for not minding me. That will do you good! As long as time lasts you shall always look like that, Birch-Tree; always be marked as one who will not mind its maker. Yes, and all the Birch-Trees in the world shall have the same marks forever.' They do, too. You have seen them and have wondered why the Birch-Tree is so queerly marked. Now you know.

"That is all — Ho!"

MISTAKES OF *OLD*–MAN

MISTAKES OF *OLD*-MAN

A LL night the storm raged, and in the morning the plains were white with snow. The sun came and the light was blinding, but the hunters were abroad early, as usual.

That day the children came to my camp, and I told them several stories that appeal to white children. They were deeply interested, and asked many questions. Not until the hunters returned did my visitors leave.

That night War Eagle told us of the mistakes of *Old*-man. He said:

"*Old*-man made a great many mistakes in making things in the world, but he worked until he had everything good. I told you at the beginning that *Old*-man made mistakes, but I didn't tell you what they were, so now I shall tell you.

"One of the things he did that was wrong, was to make the Big-Horn to live on the plains. Yes, he made him on the plains and turned him loose, to make his living there. Of course the Big-Horn couldn't run on the plains, and *Old*-man wondered what was wrong. Finally, he said: 'Come here, Big-Horn!' and the Big-Horn came to him. *Old*-man stuck his arm through the circle his horns made, and dragged the Big-Horn far up into the mountains. There he set him free again, and sat down to watch him. Ho! It made *Old*-man dizzy to watch the Big-Horn run about on the ragged cliffs. He saw at once that this was the country the Big-Horn liked, and he left him there. Yes, he left him there forever, and there he stays, seldom coming down to the lower country.

"While *Old*-man was waiting to see what the Big-Horn would do in the high mountains, he made an Antelope and set him free with the Big-Horn. Ho! But the Antelope stumbled and fell down among the rocks. He couldn't run at all; could hardly stand up. So *Old*-man called to the Antelope to come back to him, and the Antelope did come to him. Then he called to the Big-Horn, and said:

"'You are all right, I guess, but this one isn't, and I 'll have to take him somewhere else.'

"He dragged the Antelope down to the prairie country, and set him free there. Then he watched him a minute; that was as long as the Antelope was in sight, for he was afraid *Old*-man might take him back to the mountains.

"He said: 'I guess that fellow was made for the plains, all right, so I 'll leave him there'; and he did. That is why the Antelope always stays on the plains, even to-day. He likes it better.

"That wasn't a very long story; sometime when you get older I will tell you some different stories, but that will be all for this time, I guess. Ho!"

HOW THE MAN FOUND HIS MATE

HOW THE MAN FOUND HIS MATE

EACH tribe has its own stories. Most of them deal with the same subjects, differing only in immaterial particulars.

Instead of squirrels in the timber, the Blackfeet are sure they were prairie-dogs that *Old*-man roasted that time when he made the mountain-lion long and lean. The Chippewas and Crees insist that they were squirrels that were cooked and eaten, but one tribe is essentially a forest-people and the other lives on the plains — hence the difference.

Some tribes will not wear the feathers of the owl, nor will they have anything to do with that bird, while others use his feathers freely.

The forest Indian wears the soft-soled moccasin, while his brother of the plains covers the bottoms of his footwear with rawhide, because of the cactus and prickly-pear, most likely.

The door of the lodge of the forest Indian reaches to the ground, but the plains Indian makes his lodge skin to reach all about the circle at the bottom, because of the wind.

One night in War Eagle's lodge, Otherperson asked: "Why don't the Bear have a tail, grandfather?"

War Eagle laughed and said: "Our people do not know why, but we believe he was made that way at the beginning, although I have heard men of other tribes say that the Bear lost his tail while fishing.

"I don't know how true it is, but I have been told that a long time ago the Bear was fishing in the winter, and the Fox asked him if he had any luck.

"'No,' replied the Bear, 'I can't catch a fish.'

"'Well,' said the Fox, 'if you will stick your long tail down through this hole in the ice, and sit very still, I am sure you will catch a fish.'

"So the Bear stuck his tail through the hole in the ice, and the Fox told him to sit still, till he called him; then the Fox went off, pretending to hunt along the bank. It was mighty cold weather, and the water froze all about the Bear's tail, yet he sat still, waiting for the Fox to call him. Yes, the Bear sat so still and so long that his tail was frozen in the ice, but he didn't know it. When the Fox thought it was time, he called:

"'Hey, Bear, come here quick — quick! I have a Rabbit in this hole, and I want you to help me dig him out.' Ho! The Bear tried to get up, but he couldn't.

"'Hey, Bear, come here — there are two Rabbits in this hole,' called the Fox.

"The Bear pulled so hard to get away from the ice, that he broke his tail off short to his body. Then the Fox ran away laughing at the Bear.

"I hardly believe that story, but once I heard an old man who visited my father from the country far east of here, tell it. I remembered it. But I can't say that I know it is true, as I can the others.

"When I told you the story of how *Old*-man made the world over, after the water had made its war upon it, I told you how the first man and woman were made. There is another story of how the first man found his wife, and I will tell you that.

"After *Old*-man had made a man to look like himself, he left him to live with the Wolves, and went away. The man had a hard time of it, with no clothes to keep him warm, and no wife to help him, so he went out looking for *Old*-man.

"It took the man a long time to find *Old*-man's lodge, but as soon as he got there he went right in and said:

"'*Old*-man, you have made me and left me to live with the Wolf-people. I don't like them at all. They give me scraps of meat to eat and won't build a fire. They have wives,

216

but I don't want a Wolf-woman. I think you should take better care of me.'

"'Well,' replied *Old*-man, 'I was just waiting for you to come to see me. I have things fixed for you. You go down this river until you come to a steep hillside. There you will see a lodge. Then I will leave you to do the rest. Go!'

"The man started and travelled all that day. When night came he camped and ate some berries that grew near the river. The next morning he started down the river again, looking for the steep hillside and the lodge. Just before sundown, the man saw a fine lodge near a steep hillside, and he knew that was the lodge he was looking for; so he crossed the river and went into the lodge.

"Sitting by the fire inside, was a woman. She was dressed in buckskin clothes, and was cooking some meat that smelled good to the man, but when she saw him without any clothes, she pushed him out of the lodge, and dropped the door.

"Things didn't look very good to that man, I tell you, but to get even with the woman, he went up on the steep hillside and commenced to roll big rocks down upon her lodge. He kept this up until one of the largest rocks knocked down the lodge, and the woman ran out, crying.

"When the man heard the woman crying, it made him sorry and he ran down the hill to her. She sat down on the ground, and the man ran to where she was and said:

"'I am sorry I made you cry, woman. I will help you fix your lodge. I will stay with you, if you will only let me.'

"That pleased the woman, and she showed the man how to fix up the lodge and gather some wood for the fire. Then she let him come inside and eat. Finally, she made him some clothes, and they got along very well, after that.

"That is how the man found his wife — Ho!"

DREAMS

DREAMS

A S soon as manhood is attained, the young Indian must secure his "charm," or "medicine." After a sweat-bath, he retires to some lonely spot, and there, for four days and nights, if necessary, he remains in solitude. During this time he eats nothing; drinks nothing; but spends his time invoking the Great Mystery for the boon of a long life. In this state of mind, he at last sleeps, perhaps dreams. If a dream does not come to him, he abandons the task for a time, and later on will take another sweat-bath and try again. Sometimes dangerous cliffs, or other equally uncomfortable places, are selected for dreaming, because the surrounding terrors impress themselves upon the mind, and even in slumber add to the vividness of dreams.

At last the dream comes, and in it some bird
or animal appears as a helper to the dreamer,
in trouble. Then he seeks that bird or animal;
kills a specimen; and if a bird, he stuffs its skin
with moss and forever keeps it near him. If
an animal, instead of a bird, appears in the
dream, the Indian takes his hide, claws, or teeth;
and throughout his life never leaves it behind
him, unless in another dream a greater charm
is offered. If this happens, he discards the old
"medicine" for the new; but such cases are rare.

Sometimes the Indian will deck his "medicine-bundle" with fanciful trinkets and quill-
work. At other times the "bundle" is kept
forever out of the sight of all uninterested per-
sons, and is altogether unadorned. But "medicine" is necessary; without it, the Indian is
afraid of his shadow.

An old chief, who had been in many battles,
once told me his great dream, withholding the
name of the animal or bird that appeared therein
and became his "medicine."

He said that when he was a boy of twelve years, his father, who was chief of his tribe, told him that it was time that he tried to dream. After his sweat-bath, the boy followed his father without speaking, because the postulant must not converse or associate with other humans between the taking of the bath and the finished attempt to dream. On and on into the dark forest the father led, followed by the naked boy, till at last the father stopped on a high hill, at the foot of a giant pine-tree.

By signs the father told the boy to climb the tree and to get into an eagle's nest that was on the topmost boughs. Then the old man went away, in order that the boy might reach the nest without coming too close to his human conductor.

Obediently the boy climbed the tree and sat upon the eagle's nest on the top. "I could see very far from that nest," he told me. "The day was warm and I hoped to dream that night, but the wind rocked the tree top, and the darkness made me so much afraid that I did not sleep.

"On the fourth night there came a terrible thunder-storm, with lightning and much wind. The great pine groaned and shook until I was sure it must fall. All about it, equally strong trees went down with loud crashings, and in the dark there were many awful sounds — sounds that I sometimes hear yet. Rain came, and I grew cold and more afraid. I had eaten nothing, of course, and I was weak — so weak and tired, that at last I slept, in the nest. I dreamed; yes, it was a wonderful dream that came to me, and it has most all come to pass. Part is yet to come. But come it surely will.

"First I saw my own people in three wars. Then I saw the Buffalo disappear in a hole in the ground, followed by many of my people. Then I saw the whole world at war, and many flags of white men were in this land of ours. It was a terrible war, and the fighting and the blood made me sick in my dream. Then, last of all,

I saw a 'person' coming — coming across what seemed the plains. There were deep shadows all about him as he approached. This 'person' kept beckoning me to come to him, and at last I did go to him.

"'Do you know who I am,' he asked me.

"'No, "person," I do not know you. Who are you, and where is your country?'

"'If you will listen to me, boy, you shall be a great chief and your people shall love you. If you do not listen, then I shall turn against you. My name is "Reason."'

"As the 'person' spoke this last, he struck the ground with a stick he carried, and the blow set the grass afire. I have always tried to know that 'person.' I think I know him wherever he may be, and in any camp. He has helped me all my life, and I shall never turn against him — never."

That was the old chief's dream and now a word about the sweat-bath. A small lodge is made of willows, by bending them and sticking the ends in the ground. A completed sweat-lodge is shaped like an inverted bowl, and in the centre is a small hole in the ground. The lodge is covered with robes, bark, and dirt, or anything that will make it reasonably tight. Then a fire is built outside and near the sweat-lodge, in which stones are heated. When the stones are ready, the bather crawls inside the sweat-lodge, and an assistant rolls the hot stones from the fire, and into the lodge. They are then rolled into the hole in the lodge and sprinkled with water. One cannot imagine a hotter vapor bath than this system produces, and when the bather has satisfied himself inside, he darts from the sweat-lodge into the river, winter or summer. This treatment killed thousands of Indians when the smallpox was brought to them from Saint Louis, in the early days.

That night in the lodge War Eagle told a queer yarn. I shall modify it somewhat, but in our own sacred history there is a similar tale, well known to all. He said:

"Once, a long time ago, two 'thunders' were travelling in the air. They came over a village of our people, and there stopped to look about.

"In this village there was one fine, painted lodge, and in it there was an old man, an aged woman, and a beautiful young woman with wonderful hair. Of course the 'thunders' could look through the lodge skin and see all that was inside. One of them said to the other: 'Let us marry that young woman, and never tell her about it.'

"'All right,' replied the other 'thunder.' 'I am willing, for she is the finest young woman in all the village. She is good in her heart, and she is honest.'

"So they married her, without telling her about it, and she became the mother of twin boys. When these boys were born, they sat up and told their mother and the other people that they were not people, but were 'thunders,' and that they would grow up quickly.

"'When we shall have been on earth a while, we shall marry, and stay until we each have four sons of our own, then we shall go away and again become "thunders,"' they said.

"It all came to pass, just as they said it would. When they had married good women and each had four sons, they told the people one day that it was time for them to go away forever.

"There was much sorrow among the people, for the twins were good men and taught many good things which we have never forgotten, but everybody knew it had to be as they said. While they lived with us, these twins could heal the sick and tell just what was going to happen on earth.

"One day at noon the twins dressed themselves in their finest clothes and went out to a park in the forest. All the people followed them and saw them lie down on the ground in the park. The people stayed in the timber that grew about the edge of the park, and watched them until clouds and mists gathered about and hid them from view.

"It thundered loudly and the winds blew; trees fell down; and when the mists and clouds cleared away, they were gone — gone forever. But the people have never forgotten them, and my grandfather, who is in the ground near Rocker, was a descendant from one of the sons of the 'thunders.' Ho!"

RETROSPECTION

RETROSPECTION

IT was evening in the bad-lands, and the red sun had slipped behind the far-off hills. The sundown breeze bent the grasses in the coulées, and curled tiny dust-clouds on the barren knolls. Down in a gulch a clear, cool creek dallied its way toward the Missouri, where its water, bitter as gall, would be lost in the great stream. Here, where Nature forbids man to work his will, and where the she wolf dens and kills to feed her litter, an aged Indian stood near the scattered bones of two great buffalo-bulls. Time had bleached the skulls and whitened the old warrior's hair, but in the solitude he spoke to the bones as to a boyhood friend:

"Ho! Buffalo, the years are long since you died, and your tribe, like mine, was even then

233

shrinking fast, but you did not know it; would
not believe it; though the signs did not lie.
My father and his father knew your people,
and when one night you went away, we thought
you did but hide and would soon come back.
The snows have come and gone many times
since then, and still your people stay away.
The young-men say that the great herds have
gone to the Sand Hills, and that my father still
has meat. They have told me that the white
man, in his greed, has killed — and not for
meat — all the Buffalo that our people knew.
They have said that the great herds that made
the ground tremble as they ran were slain in
a few short years by those who needed not.
Can this be true, when ever since there was a
world, our people killed your kind, and still
left herds that grew in numbers until they
often blocked the rivers when they passed?
Our people killed your kind that they themselves might live, but never did they go to war
against you. Tell me, do your people hide, or

are the young-men speaking truth, and have your people gone with mine to Sand Hill shadows to come back no more?"

"Ho! red man — my people all have gone. The young-men tell the truth and all my tribe have gone to feed among the shadow-hills, and your father still has meat. My people suffer from his arrows and his lance, yet there the herds increase as they did here, until the white man came and made his war upon us without cause or need. I was one of the last to die, and with my brother here fled to this forbidding country that I might hide; but one day when the snow was on the world, a white murderer followed on our trail, and with his noisy weapon sent our spirits to join the great shadow-herds. Meat? No, he took no meat, but from our quivering flesh he tore away the robes that Napa gave to make us warm, and left us for the Wolves. That night they came, and quarrelling, fighting, snapping 'mong themselves, left but our bones to greet the morning sun.

These bones the Coyotes and the weaker ones did drag and scrape, and scrape again, until the last of flesh or muscle disappeared. Then the winds came and sang — and all was done."

The Stories in Verse

INTRODUCTION TO THE STORIES IN VERSE

Sarah Waller Hatfield

Frank Bird Linderman wrote his first-known poem, "A School Boy's Reflections," as a young boy living in Elyria and Lorain, Ohio. The poem shows his disdain for both organized school and his brother, Percy, the teacher's pet. The poem is perhaps a prelude of Linderman's restless spirit and desire to learn in unconventional ways. This creative expression, however, is apparent in the more than two hundred known poems Linderman wrote throughout his life (1869–1938).

A School Boy's Reflections

SCHOOL

The Hist'ry says this country's free,
And mother says so too,
And pop, he says "you bet it is,"
So course it must be true.
But if it is why do they make
All children go to school?
I 'ist say "yes" when mother asks
If I'd like to be a fool.
An' I would.

THE STORIES IN VERSE

THE TEACHER

But school would not be half so bad
If teachers had some sense,
The one that us kids has got now
Is like a stiff board fence.
An' when you get up to recite
An' kind of feel aroun'
An' say that two times two is five
Why she 'ist says "Sit down."
An' I do.

REPORTS

Another mean thing teacher does
Is makin' out reports;
She always gives the lowest marks
To boys what are the sports;
And Percy gets the highest ones
Just like all teacher's pets.
I wouldn't be that sissy boy
For all the marks he gets.
An' that's so.

It is not known for certain when the thirteen poems
that are appearing for the first time in this new edition of *Indian Why Stories* were first written by Frank
Linderman. The poems match some of the Blackfeet,
Chippewa (Ojibwa), and Cree legends published in his
first book, *Indian Why Stories: Sparks from War Eagle's
Lodge-Fire* (Scribners 1915, illustrated by Charles M.
Russell). There is no better person than Frank to tell,
in his own words, what led him to record these poems.

THE STORIES IN VERSE

In a March 12, 1918, letter written to a Mrs. Roberts he said:

I came to Montana when I was a boy of 17 and Fortune directed my way to its wildest portion, the Flathead country, where I trapped and hunted for nearly seven years. During all of this time I was among the Flatheads and Kootenais who have always inhabited this section. In 1885 the Riel Rebellion was added to the history of the Northwest and after some desperate fighting the Crees and Chippewas were beaten by the Canadian troops. These Indians came across the line into Montana and some thirty lodges of them camped near me in the Flathead. They were pictures in extreme and full of fight. I soon learned that they were wholly unspoiled by contact with the white man. They clung to their old customs and traditions more closely than did the Flatheads or Kootenais because the latter had been associated with the "black-robes" and other missionaries for many years. The chiefs—there were two of them—Cree Chief Little Bear, and an old Medicine-man, whose name was "Full-of-dew," became fast friends of mine and from them all, especially the latter, I learned much of the "long ago." I had had trouble with the Kootenais and even to this day I have not quite forgiven them so I sought to strengthen the friendship between the new arrivals and myself. This friendship has lasted unbroken since 1885. In fact I am a Chippewa by adoption and as the Crees and Chippewas claim kinship and have always been allies, I feel myself to be as much a Cree as a Chippewa. The band of Chippewas that had taken the war over the border had drifted to the buffalo range from Wisconsin many years before but they had frequented the plains always. You will find that these people drove the great Sioux tribes to the Dakotas from the head of Lake Superior in "Sixteen hun-

241

THE STORIES IN VERSE

dred and something" where they have since lived. At the beginning I found the whiteman who know most of the redmen, knew but little. The ideas possessed by them were seldom correct. This was especially true of the men who had taken Indian wives and settled among the tribes of the plains and mountains. I had been a collector of stone arrow-points at home in Ohio and after reading "Atlantis" I became convinced that if the Indian ever used these it was hundreds of years ago. I think this idea was largely responsible for my trying to learn of the folk-lore of the Indian. I soon satisfied myself the stone arrow-point belonged to some other race than the Indian but in arriving at this decision I ran across many stories which I thought worth saving. I was careful in securing these stories and tried many individuals among the older Indians I knew but found them to be as careful as myself in handling them. They differed somewhat at times but in the main were alike. In the work of gathering the legends I became interested in the Indian's religion and found much worth knowing. I admire the Indian. I mean the old Indian; not the young, moving-picture Indian but the real unspoiled man of the wilds. He is the only human I have ever known who knows no jealousy. He will ever extol the prowess of the competitor who beats him at any game or trial of skill. The successful man is not envied but is pointed to with pride by his fellows. I have tried to know him for over 33 years and while he has called me brother and friend I feel that I have learned but little of this man of mystery—the Indian.

In his autobiography, *Montana Adventure: Recollections of Frank B. Linderman*, edited by Harold G. Merriam (University of Nebraska Press, 1968), Linderman relates a story from 1889 when he was guiding a group

THE STORIES IN VERSE

of prominent Montanans—former territorial governor Sam Hauser, Judge Woody, G. A. Wolf of Missoula, and Hon. A. Sterne Blake. They advised him, "You don't belong in the wilds . . . when you come out of the wilderness look us up, any of us. We'll help you get your stride, some way."

By the time he quit the "free life" in 1891 and had married Minnie Johns in 1893, he had gathered a wealth of facts from his Indian friends that provided fodder for his later work as an author, lecturer, and sculptor. He first worked as a bookkeeper and then as a self-taught chemist-assayer at the Curlew Mine in Victor, Montana, an enterprise owned in part by A. Sterne Blake.

We now know that young Frank Linderman, while struggling to support his wife by working at the Curlew Mine, was also already at work writing about what he had learned from his Indian friends. On January 16, 1963, Mrs. Monterey Leach of Billings (Blake's granddaughter), wrote to Norma Waller, Frank Linderman's daughter:

I am writing you to tell you how much I enjoyed the article in the Montana magazine. . . . I was especially interested, because it mentioned my grandfather, A. Sterne Blake. I've heard my mother, Julia Blake Yates tell about your father working at the Curlew Mines, and he stayed with the Blake family in Victor at the time. My mother was a young girl at the time, but she told me how she used to make up Mr. Linderman's room and take a peek at his writings. Little did she know then, that his wonderful articles and books would be published for us to read and enjoy. At the time your father stayed there, my grandfather had a part interest in the mines.

243

THE STORIES IN VERSE

In the article in *Montana Adventure*, Frank reveals the close kinship he felt for his Indian friends and his ultimate destiny when he discovered four Indian lodges near the foothills outside of Butte around 1896:

> The sight of them thrilled me more than anything I had lately seen. The day was fine. The mountain-tops laid shadows upon the four lodges that seemed to belong to another world altogether. I walked to the camp, not guessing what Indians were there. Imagine my delight when I was greeted by my old friend, Muskegon, the Cree, who had told me so many tribal folk tales in the Flathead. . . . I did not then suspect that the wandering band of Crees and Chippewas, numbering about three hundred men, women and children, to which these four lodges belonged, would someday become a charge of mine.

The band, which had taken part in the Riel Rebellion in Saskatchewan in 1885 and was befriended by tenderfoot Frank Linderman, had been wandering in poverty and distress since the revolt. They continued as homeless Indians until Linderman successfully got the Rocky Boy Reservation established for them at Box Elder in 1916 after an extensive eight-year appeal with the help of influential Montanans like Paris Gibson, founder of Great Falls, and Charles Russell. Linderman spearheaded the gathering of food and clothing for the destitute Indians, who had become his charges— they were even dubbed "Linderman Indians." Because of his continued help, many Indians in return showered him with their prized artifacts, and beaded or quilled clothing as tokens of their trust and appreciation. Linderman tells one story when Full-of-dew (Pah-nah-to) stripped off his beaded clothing in Linderman's Helena office to give it to him because the starving Chippewa

THE STORIES IN VERSE

had killed and eaten a horse that Linderman had given to him as a gift.

In March of 1899 Linderman bought the *Sheridan Chinook* newspaper on a dare—five dollars down, plus a mortgage—and learned to set type. His writings, the result of filling sixteen columns each week—became an important part of his life's work.

Thirteen of the legends told by War-Eagle (Chief Full-of-dew) and reprinted in Linderman's *Indian Why Stories* are assumed to have been written in verse form sometime between 1885 and before 1915, because their titles differ slightly and a specific poem does not exist for every published legend. Yet the poems are historically important renderings, not only for their charm but also because several tribes are identified in the titles, such as "How the Old-man Made the World Over (Chippewa Tale)," "Why the Panther Wears Singed Hair and Is Lean and Long (Blackfeet Story)," and "Why the Birch Tree Wears Slashes in Its Bark (Blackfeet Story)."

Although the poem "How the Otter Skin Became Great Medicine" cannot be attributed to a specific tribe, it is undoubtedly a Cree tale written after Linderman and Charles Russell attended a Cree Sundance at Fort Browning in 1912. Their attendance at the Sundance lends further credence to the belief that the poetry versions of the legends were written before the book. Linderman recorded the encounter at the ceremony in the story in *Montana Adventure* and in more detail in his *Recollections of Charley Russell*, edited by H. G. Merriam (University of Oklahoma Press, 1964).

> The drums, several of them, beating in unison sounded savagely forbidding. Nevertheless, I lifted the canvas door and entered, followed by the others.

THE STORIES IN VERSE

The drums ceased, heads turned, angry eyes glared. In a jiffy Little-bear, the Cree chief, clad only a breech clout, sprang toward us, speaking rapidly in Cree. But he stopped as suddenly as he had started, a broad, happy smile lighting his powerful face.

"How! How!" he greeted; then, turning to his people. "My brother has come to us. My heart sings," he said, going on with a long speech of welcome.

Finishing, he strode majestically to the center pole of the sun lodge where two or three pieces of finery, "medicine" were hanging, lifted down an old otter skin (bedecked with eagle feathers, hawk bells and medicine) and handed it to me, saying: "This belonged to my grandfather, my father and me. I now give it to you. Hold it fast. It is big medicine."

Frank Linderman and Charles Russell first met in the mid-1890s, and remained lifelong friends. They visited one another's homes, and sometimes Linderman would observe in silence as Russell painted in his Great Falls studio. They inspired each other as they reminisced or recorded the vanishing life of the West in their individual art forms. The men's friendship was well established when Frank wrote his wife on October 25, 1908, from Great Falls:

Dear Frau:
Been here checking up entries in U. S. Land office, and waiting for partner to return from Helena. Costing me something to stay but Russell and I have smoked the big pipe and are good tillicums now so I guess the time is well spent. This morning we got out a wooden model of a pack horse and threw the <> hitch in all its ways, much to the satisfaction of ourselves and friends. He wants to take my poems to New York this winter. We are 2 of a kind Russell and I and I believe that it was "in the cards" to meet as we

246

THE STORIES IN VERSE

did. In fact Min, I believe that the cards are stacked for me and they'll play themselves. . . . Be a good girl and ask me what I saw in Russell's cabin when I get to camp. . . . Yours Frank.

On January 21, 1921, Frank also wrote to W. H. Murgitroyd of Spokane, Washington, about the progress of the book's publication:

I have just returned from Helena where I have been interviewing and being interviewed by different publishers from the East.

I believe things will move a little smoother for me from now on because two of the biggest publishing houses seemed to be bidding against each other for some of my stuff, especially poetry.

There is no record if Russell ever did take Linderman's poems to New York. A group of poems that intrigued Russell might have included the verse version of Linderman's first *Indian Why Stories*, or some of the poems published in August of 1921 in his *Bunch Grass and Blue Joint* (Scribner & Sons, 1920), such as these three (excerpted):

The Lonely Tepee

Alone on the sage-brush stretches
here roamed the bison herds,
And rules a race of warriors
Free as the flight of birds—
This ghost of old-time greatness
In twilight of the past,
The remnant of a shadow
Now dim, and fading fast.

247

THE STORIES IN VERSE

Cabins

They was dirt-roofed, an' homely, an' ramblin', an'
squat—
Jest logs with mud-daubin'; but I loved 'em a lot.
Their latch-strings was out, an' their door wouldn't
lock:
Get down an' walk in ('twas politer to knock).
Mebby nobody home, but the grub was all there;
He'p yerse'f, leave a note, to show you was square;
Might be gone for a week; stay as long as you please,
You knowed you was welcome as a cool summer breeze;
Might be spring 'fore you'd see him, then he'd grin an'
declare
He'd a-give a good hoss if he'd only been there.

The Council of the Sun

Once when night had spread her blanket
O'er the prairies and the hills.
And the Moon was watching over
Mighty streams and tiny rills.

Slept the Sun within his teepee,
Where the great West wind was born;
Slept and dreamed he of his people,
Till he felt the coming morn.

Then he rose and pondered deeply,
For a blood hand had crept
Toward his people from the eastward:
He had dreamed it as he slept.

THE STORIES IN VERSE

"This," said he, "must mean extinction
For my people and their ways;
Means the buffalo will vanish,
With the lore of other days."

. . . .

Hid he there, my muskrat cousin;
Learned he much of Whitemen's ways;

. . . .

Then he told me of a Young-man
Who made picture-stories true,
of the Redman's life and battles;
of our hills and rivers, too.

Told me that with brush and colors
made he stories of the fight;
of the hunt, and of our people;
Of the daytime and the night.

"Great, O Sun, this story-teller,
Running Antelope, his name;
Let us make him chief among us,
Let us feed his fire with flame."

. . . .

–Note: Running Antelope is a name given to Charles Russell
by the Blackfeet.

The Blackfeet, Flathead, a few of the more warlike
Kootenai, and, years later, the Crows were Linderman's
friends. He devoted much of his life learning and making written record of legends from the various tribes,
and was always ready to help in a material way whenever he could. Linderman was adopted into three tribes:

249

THE STORIES IN VERSE

the Blackfeet named him Mex-skim-yo-peek-kinny, or Iron Tooth; the Crees called him Co-skee-see-co-cot, meaning The Man Who Looks Through Glasses (some older Crees called him Sings Like a Bird); and the Crows gave him the name Mah-paht-sa-not-tsasa, or Great Sign Talker.

Linderman trusted only full-bloods like his Cree friends Muskegon and Little Bear, old Chippewas such as Full-of-dew and Big Rock, the Kootenai Two-Comes-Over-the-Hill, and the Crows' Chief Plenty-Coups and the medicine woman Pretty-Shield for accurate accounts of their legends, traditional customs, and rites.

Linderman honored his many Indian friends through his writings. His poem, "Little Bear, Chief of the Crees," was published both in *Indian Why Stories* and in his book of poetry, *Bunch Grass and Blue Joint*. Furthermore, he created several sculptures of Chief Little Bear as a testimonial to their friendship.

Full-of-dew was personified in Linderman's stories as War Eagle, the grandfather telling stories around the nightly teepee fire about the "whys" and "hows" of the birds and animals. It is continually evident, in archival writings and in the words of his descendants, that in Linderman's early days his Indian friends revered him; they continue to honor and credit him with saving their cultural lore, and in some cases say he is the very reason they even exist today.

In a letter written in 1931, Day Child, a Cree Indian, expressed his indebtedness to Frank Linderman:

Dear Mr. Linderman:
I am thinking of You today Why? its because you are the Man that got this Reservation for us. And all of the Rocky Boy Indians are thanking you.

THE STORIES IN VERSE

Day Child also wrote in another letter:

> I want you to know how I like Frank Linderman. My father
> is dead. I loved him, but if my father came back and stood
> on one hill and I saw Frank Linderman on another hill I
> would not go to my father, I would go to Frank Linderman.
> You know I do not lie. This is the Truth.

In *Montana Adventure* Linderman states that Full-
of-dew was a profound mystic. Frank asked him: "Who
is Manitou?"

> He looked about, his eyes settling for a moment on the
> far mountains white with snow. "The mountains, the low-
> lands, the rivers, the birds, my fire, the people, the big
> trees" he said slowly. Then he added, "believe that the big
> trees speak to you, Co-skee-see-co-cot, but not to many
> other white men."

In 2002 the granddaughter of Full-of-dew (Pah-nah-
to), Nadine Ironmaker Morsette, who lives on the Rocky
Boy Reservation, brought a photograph of Full-of-dew
and his wife, Prairie Dog (Chi-pos-ki-si-s), to be exhib-
ited in the Linderman exhibit at the Museum at Cen-
tral School. Morsette said Pah-nah-to's name was not
Full-of-dew, and that the name was simply one Linderman had given him, just as Linderman had cast him as
War Eagle.

Descendants of Loud Thunder (Chippewa) and Medicine-man (Big Rock), who gave Linderman stories of
creation for *Indian Old-Man Stories: More Sparks from
War Eagle's Lodge-Fire*, credit him with offering proof
of how a rare thirteen-star U.S. flag was presented to
their ancestors nearly two hundred years ago. When
Linderman attended a Cree Sundance in 1933, he was

251

THE STORIES IN VERSE

shown the flag by an old Chippewa Indian from Canada named Frenchman, who was passing ownership to his nephew, Loud Thunder. Frenchman told Linderman the history of the flag, and allowed him to have his picture taken holding the flag with Loud Thunder. Linderman later recorded the story in "Who Was this Soldier Chief?" which was published in 1934 in the *American Legion Magazine*. These are some of the Indians who feel they would not be alive today had Linderman not helped save their ancestors from starvation. To this day they honor him at cultural Round Dances.

In 1994 John Well-off-man, a Chippewa-Cree artist from Rocky Boy Reservation, said the Indians gave Frank Linderman their stories to honor him the way the white man bestows an honorary degree. The sharing of stories is a bigger honor than just giving an Indian name. Well-off-man stated that when times were hard for the Indians, Linderman stood with them against opposition. Linderman knew what it was like to get up in the morning and give thanks to the Creator, so the Indians honored him by giving him their stories of creation.

On June 18, 1922, Linderman wrote to Harry Cunningham in Helena about Cunningham's offer to return to the life insurance business:

> Your offer is magnanimous . . . but up to now I have not thought of lessening my literary efforts for I am getting along fairly well and my books are being well received. I found long ago that I could not write books and life insurance, and while I am sure that I could earn more money at the latter game I have long ago determined that there are more worth while things than dollars. It is hard for some of my friends to believe that I feel it a duty to, in some way,

252

THE STORIES IN VERSE

preserve the old West, especially Montana, in printers ink and if I can only accomplish a small part of that duty I shall die contented . . . as Mark Twain has said, "I know I am a fool but I am God Almighty's fool and his works must be respected."

Frank Bird Linderman was a poet by instinct. He listened to that "inner voice" and never turned his back on his literary career. In every poem or book he has honored the Indian friends who trusted him.

THE STORIES IN VERSE

Frank Bird Linderman

HOW THE DUCK-PEOPLE GOT THEIR
PRETTY FEATHERS

'Twas in fall and winds that warn us
Of the winter shook the trees.
Yellow leaves on quaking aspens
Rattled in the chilling breeze.

On the streams the summer clothing
Of the birch and alder sailed,
And the *buck*-deer from the ridges
To the lower country trailed.

On a lake the ducks were playing;
Laughing loudly in their glee;
Loons were calling, swimming, diving;
'Twas a merry sight to see.

Old-man saw them from a hill-top;
Took some moss and made a ball;
Very large he rolled and made it,
Then began to cry and call:

THE STORIES IN VERSE

"Ho! My brothers, do not frighten;
Come and let us dance and play;
See, I have a load to carry;
Great it is and rough the way."

Said the grey-goose, "Do not heed him;
Bad the *Old*-man's heart and mind;
He will fool us if we let him
For his deeds are seldom kind."

On the shore the *Old*-man begged them;
Made a fire and stories told;
Turned the moss-ball o'er and over,
Till at last it was unrolled.

Near the land the ducks had wandered;
Watched the *Old*-man build a lodge
Of the moss and poles he'd gathered,
Each alert a stone to dodge.

All about the fire the *Old*-man
Built the lodge; then beat his drum,
Chanting slowly in the duck-talk,
Words inviting them to come.

Shyly to the lodge they waddled,
Laying fear aside at last;
Gained the inside of the tepee;
Smoked the pipe when it was passed.

Spake the *Old*-man, "Now I'll paint you
For the Blind-dance of your race;

256

THE STORIES IN VERSE

Brother Mallard, name the colors
For your breast and neck and face."

"Green of head, with snowy circle
On my neck," the drake replied.
"Make my breast of brown the richest,
Use some black and white beside."

Blue-winded teal and gaudy wood-duck;
Loon and blue-bill, goose and brant—
Each one chose the paint that pleased him;
Old-man worked nor ceased his chant.

Fire-light shone on brightest colors
When the *Old*-man's work was done;
"Now," said he, "we'll dance the Blind-dance.
Ho!—'twill be a night of fun."

"All must shut their eyes and circle
Past me as I beat the drum—
'Round the fire!" And then he chanted,
"Now you come ducks—now you come."

'Round they circled to the *Old*-man
When he'd seize them as they'd pass,
Wring their necks and throw their bodies
Out upon the weeds and grass.

Many died but in the door-way
Loon had stopped and peeked an eye—
Saw the wicked work of *Old*-man;
Cried, "He's killing us—let's fly."

257

THE STORIES IN VERSE

Quacked the drakes and honked the ganders
As they fled from out the lodge.
Old-man kicked the back of Loon-duck,
Though he ran and tried to dodge.

That is why the loon is clumsy
In his walk upon the land—
Why his feet turn from his body
When he walks or tries to stand.

All the ducks that peeked at *Old*-man,
Have red eyes—he made them sore;
Red they stay to pay for peeking,
But they smart and hurt no more.

And the colors *Old*-man painted,
Stand today, as you may see,
Just as they were made for dancing;
Clear and brilliant as can be.

WHY THE KINGFISHER WEARS A TOP-KNOT
(An Indian Legend)

Have I told you why King-fisher
Top-knot wears like men in War;
Why he always wears a Head-dress;
Sought you n'er the reason for?

Young-man listen; I will tell you.
Long ago it was and cold,
And my father was a young man;
Long he's dead and I am old.

258

THE STORIES IN VERSE

'Twas in winter when the *Old*-man
And his brother Wolf, they say,
Sought for meat along the river;
Deep the snow and cold the day.

Thick the ice upon the river;
Game had fled before the snow,
To the lowlands and the valleys
Where the snowstorms do not go.

War there was between their people
And the Crow Tribe on the plain,
Thus they feared to hunt the valley
Lest they n'er return again.

Saw the otter on the river;
Saw them run and dance and play;
Saw them slide into the water
Through the holes along the way.

Holes the water makes in passing;
For the fish the holes are made,
That they breathe there in the water,
When on all the ice is laid.

"I am swift of foot," the wolf said;
"Sharp my teeth and very strong:
Stand you here—I'll catch an otter
Wait you here—'twill not be long."

Then the wolf upon the river
Stepped and ran in headlong race

THE STORIES IN VERSE

Slipped he much and in his running
Made a very funny chase.

Ran the wolf until the otter
Gained a sun-hole in the ice;
In they went—the wolf in after,
Like a weasel after mice.

Ran the *Old*-man far below them,
Fearing lest his Brother drown
Ran to where the ice had opened
And the water made a sound.

Mourned he great and long he waited;
Loud he called and beckoned too
For the wolf his little brother
Then he wailed as women do.

As he called and wailed in anguish;
From a leaning birch's limb
Where he sat and watched for fishes,
A *king*-fisher laughed at him.

Laughed and tittered at his anguish;
At the *Old*-man from the limb,
Till in anger, with his war-club
Fierce, the *Old*-man struck at him.

Swung he hard but grazed the feathers
On his head and made them stand:
Now his children wear head-dresses,
Wear War-bonnets in the land.

THE STORIES IN VERSE

WHY THE CURLEW'S BILL IS LONG AND CROOKED

Once a mighty rock was hanging,
Ready any time to fall;
'Neath the rock some mice were playing
When they heard the *Old*-man call.

They'd been running just below it;
Back and forth they scampered past;
Looking sharp that they might dodge it,
If the rock should fall at last.

Fun they had and great their laughing;
Spry they ran and always clear;
Never paused and in their running
Showed that they had naught to fear.

"Let me play," said Napa to them;
"O! Be careful," said the mice,
"Lest you shake the ground in running,"
But he heeded no advice.

Ran the *Old*-man like a grizzly;
Shook the ground and then at last—
Swow!—the rock had caught the *Old*-man,
Caught and held him 'neath it fast.

"Help me brothers," cried the *Old*-man;
But they couldn't get him out;
Then in fear at once the *Old*-man
Brought the coyote with a shout.

261

THE STORIES IN VERSE

Coyote couldn't help the *Old*-man
And a Curlew tried in vain;
Pecked the rock and tried to break it—
Pecked and tried with might and main.

Anger got the best of Napa
And he seized the Curlew's bill;
Pulled it out and bent it downward,
And he wears it that way still.

HOW THE *OLD*-MAN MADE THE WORLD OVER
(Chippewa Tale)

Once alone with bear and beaver,
Beasts and birds both great and small
Dwelt the *Old*-man, chief among them
And he called them brothers, all.

They were brothers of the *Old*-man
Much he taught them that they know;
Taught the squirrel to plant the pinenut
That another tree might grow.

Knew the lynx and mink and badger;
Taught them how to hunt and hide;
Swam with geese upon the water;
Laughed to see the otters slide.

Taught the beaver all his cunning;
How to make the water deep;
When the snow grew deep in winter,
Told the bear to go to sleep.

262

THE STORIES IN VERSE

Spoke the language of the robin;
Knew the sign-talk of the bear.
Sat with grey wolves all about him;
Smoked within the cougar's lair.

All went well for many seasons
Till at last there came a rain;
Rain in sheets and rain in torrents,
Till the streams o'ran the plain.

Great the fear that was upon them.
E'en the bear confessed his fright
To the owl, the bird of shadows;
Bird that only sees at night.

Silent stole the wolf and panther
To the council with the mouse,
Came the hawk and little sparrow,
With the eagle and the grouse.

Near the lynx there sat the rabbit,
For the fear that tamed the bear
Made the least there was among them
Equal to the greatest there.

'Round the fire they sat and listened
While the bear his story told,
And the beaver told the *Old*-man
How his dams had failed to hold.

Then they cried, O! save us *Old*-man;
Save us all or we shall drown.

THE STORIES IN VERSE

But the *Old*-man smoked and listened;
Smoked and sat upon the ground.

Long he mused amid the clamor.
Then his war-song chanted low;
Seized his mighty axe of magic,
Laid a monstrous pine tree low.

Yet another and another
Of the greatest size and length.
Ten times ten they lay before him
Bound he them with withes of strength.

Tightly with the aid of magic,
Built a raft of monstrous size.
Bade them haste to sit upon it
Ere the angry waters rise.

Swiftly crept the flood upon them.
Swung the raft in circles 'round;
Creaked and groaned the withes of willow
As the pine logs left the ground.

Rocking as though spirits shook it;
Bumping, swirling in the dark;
Turning here and there with eddies,
Like canoe that's made of bark.

'Rose the raft above the aspens;
O'er the tamarack and the pine;
O'er the ragged peaks of mountains
Ere the sun arose to shine.

THE STORIES IN VERSE

Reached the sky into the waters
Like a bowl upon the tide.
All was water, water, water,
Angry water deep and wide.

Days and days in fear they drifted,
Nights and nights beneath the moon;
Till the *Old*-man bade the chipmunk
Bring to him the spotted loon.

"Loon," he said, "you are a diver;
Deep below us lies the land;
I would make the whole world over,
If some dirt were in my hand."

"Bring me earth by diving for it
Serve thy brothers by thy skill;
Should you drown while in the water,
Life is mine to give at will."

"Life I'll give if you should lose it;
Aid me and I'll make the world."
So, in fear the loon descended
In the flood that raged and whirled.

Long he stayed beneath the water;
Then they saw him floating dead.
On the raft the *Old*-man laid him,
Blew his breath upon his head.

Life returned, and to the otter
Old-man turned and begged his aid;

THE STORIES IN VERSE

But the otter died in seeking
Dirt from which the world was made.

Tried the mink and cunning beaver;
Tried the grey goose and his wife;
Dived and died as did the others,
And the *Old*-man gave them life.

None had lived to see the tree-tops.
Gloom had settled o'er the raft;
When the muskrat meekly ventured
From the over-burdened craft.

Flip! his tail had cut the water
Ere his fellows knew his aim.
Fierce he strove to gain the bottom,
Struggled with all might and main.

Longer stayed he than the others;
Swam until the trees he spied;
Strove to reach the earth beneath them,
Struggled on until he died.

Back to life the *Old*-man brought him.
Praised him—told him he was brave:
Bring me earth O! little brother;
Try again our lives to save.

He dove again and swimming bravely
Reached the earth and grasped a mite;
Clinched it tight and turning upward,
Died long ere he reached the light.

THE STORIES IN VERSE

From his paw, the *Old*-man gently
Took the dirt—then gave him breath.
Two times more for earth he sent him;
Two times more he suffered death.

Then the *Old*-man sang his war-song;
Dried the dirt beneath his hand;
Blew his magic breath upon it;
Blew that he might make the land.

Swift it whirled upon the water,
Growing fast until the trees
Bent and swayed, like trees beneath them,
In the wondrous magic breeze.

"Wolf, my brother," called the *Old*-man
"Run you 'round the land I've made;
I must know its size, my brother;
You are swift and not afraid."

Half a year it took to travel
From the raft around the land.
"Not enough," the *Old*-man told them.
Then he blew and waved his hand.

Once again the grey wolf brother
Started on his journey 'round,
But old age had stopped his heart-beats
Ere again the raft he found.

"Good, and now I'll make a people;
Make them like I am myself."

THE STORIES IN VERSE

And some clay he quickly fashioned;
Blew his breath upon the elf.

Then he made a tiny woman,
Sat them near him side by side;
Made them grow to mighty people,
Gave them health and strength beside.

Chippewas, he called his people,
And they lived upon the land,
Happy till a white man wandered
To the wild and magic strand.

Then the white man stole the woman:
Whence the tribes come of today.
None are pure of blood but children
Of the two he made of clay.

WHY THE BLACKFEET NEVER KILL MICE

Long ago when Napa made
The animals and birds,
He gave to each the sign-talk
Which is language without words.

Bears could talk to robins:
Beavers to the fox and lynx
Bison spoke to martin,
(Pretty cousin of the mink's).

Then arose a mighty question
Which should be the greatest Chief:

THE STORIES IN VERSE

Should the place be gained by wisdom,
Or through cunning like the thief.

Long they quarreled in their councils
Each at length set forth his right.
Till at last came Napa to them,
Said he'd settle it that night.

In his hand a bone he showed them;
Taught them how to play the game
That our people, learning from them,
Play today and just the same.

Then he told them that by playing
They must win the right to lead;
Bade them then to stop their quarrel;
Bade them watch him and take heed.

Long they played until the Bison
With the Mouse played all alone.
Quick with hands, Mouse beat the Bison,
Beat him playing with the bone.

"I'm too small to be your leader
Though I've won the place tonight;
To the Man I freely give it,
And to give it is my right.

After that the Mouse built tepees
In the Bison skulls he found,
And our people never hurt him
When they see him on the ground.

THE STORIES IN VERSE

HOW THE OTTER SKIN BECAME GREAT MEDICINE

Once a *Young*-man with no people
Had no luck in war or chase;
Found no woman he could marry;
In the council had no place.

Bad his Medicine and dreaming
Though alone he often tried.
Not a dream the Sun would send him,
Till along a river's side

One day in the early summer,
Near a grove wherein he stood,
Young-man saw an aged woman
Very busy gathering wood.

"Why so sad," she asked the *Young*-man
Then he told her of his woe.
"Listen *Young*-man," said the woman,
"And I'll tell you where to go."

Then she drew from 'neath her blanket
Moccasins and sack of meat.
Take the sack she told the *Young*-man
"And the clothing for your feet."

"Listen now, a song I'll teach you,"
Soft she sang lest others hear.
Many times she sang it for him
Till the words and notes were clear.

THE STORIES IN VERSE

Till he knew the song she taught him;
Then she said, "Now you must go
Till you find a beaver village,
Then you sing quite soft and low."

"Somewhere on this very river
Lives a beaver white as snow;
Chief he is of all the beavers;
Much of magic beavers know."

"All the animals will listen;
Each will aid you when you sing;
But the Chief of all the beavers
Best can tell, how luck to bring."

In the west the Sun was hanging
When the *Young*-man started out.
Long his steps and far he traveled
For his heart was young and stout.

Then he saw a beaver village;
Great in size the lodges were.
Here he sang until a beaver
Stood before him, white of fur.

"Speak, my brother," said the beaver,
"Tell me why you sing that song."
Then the *Young*-man told his troubles;
Said his Medicine was wrong.

"Take this stick," replied the beaver,
"With it you may cross the streams;

THE STORIES IN VERSE

May not drown, for deepest water,
With the stick but shallow seems."

"Go on down this very river
Till you see upon a hill
My brother 'little coyote';
If you sing, he'll do your will."

"He will lead you then to Napa
Who is very wise they say;
He will tell you much of dreaming,
But 'tis very far away."

So the *Young*-man journeyed onward;
Ate the last he had of meat;
Drank of springs and in the water
Bathed his sore and tired feet.

Looked about and saw a coyote;
Sang the song until he came;
Then he told him what he wanted;
Asked for meat and without shame.

"Wolf, my cousin," said the coyote
"Has but lately killed a doe,
Rest you here and to my cousin
For some meat I'll gladly go."

Back the coyote came with venison
Young-man built a fire and ate,
Then with coyote *Young*-man started
For the lodge of Napa, great.

THE STORIES IN VERSE

Long they traveled in the mountains;
High they climbed till in the night,
Near a cave the coyote left him,
Silently he slipped from sight.

Fear had seized the heart of *Young*-man
For a fire burned in the cave;
In he walked and there was Napa
Mighty, solemn, old and grave.

"Sit," said Napa, "Sit and tell me
Why you sought my tepee so."
Then the *Young*-man told his troubles
And his voice was soft and low.

"Now, we'll smoke, my son," said Napa
And the pipe of magic passed.
Long they smoked there in the silence
Then 'twas Napa spoke at last.

"On the top of this great mountain
Where the storm-clouds always stay
And the snow lives on forever,
There's a Chief that knows the way."

"Knows a lot of mighty dreaming.
He's a ghost-owl and is wise;
For his people all are spirits
War-like, fierce though small of size."

"Take this bow without an arrow,
That you may appear unarmed;

273

THE STORIES IN VERSE

Go among them very bravely;
Show no fear lest you be harmed."

So the *Young*-man started upward;
Up where clouds and mist and snow
Live and never die, like people,
Up where few men like to go.

Near the top heard "little singing"
All about him heard the song;
Song of war and fierce encounter;
Strange the song and very long.

Then the wind came o'er the mountain
Parted clouds and all around
Were the fierce and ghostly people
Seated on the icy ground.

Big their heads and small of body;
Armed with shields and bows and spears
'Round an owl sat all the people
Ghost-owl, that our people fears.

Fierce with spears upon the *Young*-man
Sprang the people with a cry,
But he folded arms and told them,
"Come and see a Blackfeet die."

"Stop," the Owl said to his people;
"Kill no man when he's unarmed.
Come, my son and smoke among us,
Sit and smoke; you'll not be harmed."

THE STORIES IN VERSE

Then the *Young*-man told his troubles;
Of his journey and his song;
Of the Beaver and of Napa;
How the coyote came along.

When he'd finished and was silent,
Spoke the Ghost-owl soft and kind;
"Go you down this mighty mountain:
Go until a stream you find."

"Dark 'twill be upon the river
But you'll always know the way:
Take this arrow that I give you;
Mark you well what I shall say."

"In the water of the river,
You will hear a splashing, great.
Shoot this arrow at the splasher;
Shoot at sound and do not wait."

"You will kill the mighty splasher,
Then you take and wear his hide.
Mighty Medicine and Magic
In the skin will e're abide."

Young-man started down the mountain;
Reached the river in the dark:
Journeyed on along the river—
"What was that?" he whispered—"Hark."

'Twas a splashing in the water—
Quick he let the arrow fly

THE STORIES IN VERSE

At the sound upon the water:
Saw a mighty otter die.

With the stick the Beaver gave him,
Young-man walked into the stream;
Drew the body with him shoreward;
On the grass he skinned it clean.

In the brush a coyote waited;
Called a night-bird from the trees
As the Young-man worked at skinning
Felt the coming morning breeze.

With the skin upon his shoulder
Young-man lived till very old:
Lucky in his hunt for bison;
In the war was fierce and bold.

Great he grew among his people
Greatest Chief his people had;
All forgot the way he suffered
When his Medicine was bad.

NAPA STEALS THE SUN'S LEGGINGS

Once the Moon made Sun some leggings,
Worked with quills of porcupines;
Colored deed and very pretty,
Bearing writing done in signs.
Signs the Sun and Moon, his woman,
Know and use and never change;

THE STORIES IN VERSE

Queer in beauty and in pattern;
Big in Medicine and strange.

Proud the Sun was of his leggings
And at night when seeking rest,
Slept and used them for a pillow
In his tepee in the west.
One night Napa passed the tepee;
Saw the leggings and the Sun;
Tried to steal them from the sleeper;
Made some noise and had to run.

Hid the thief nearby the tepee
Till the Sun returned and slept;
Then, into the lodge of magic
Silently old Napa crept.
Rich the linings and the sun-robes,
Tanned and painted by the Moon.
'Mong the pines there called a night-bird;
From the river cried the loon.

Ghostly sounds made Napa shudder,
But at last he reached the bed;
Deftly stole the pretty leggings
From beneath the sleeper's head.
Then he ran and ran to Eastward;
Ran until his legs were sore;
Then with leggings for a pillow
Stretched himself to sleep and snore.

Long he slept and when he wakened,
Rested from his mighty run;

THE STORIES IN VERSE

Looking in his face and smiling
Napa saw the rising Sun.
"Ha, you thief; you stole my leggings,"
Said the Sun and Napa fled,
Left the leggings both behind him;
Left them there upon his bed.

Napa ran and going Westward,
Near the tepee, hid once more.
Stole the leggings in the darkness
Ere the Sun began to snore.
"Now," said he, "he'll never catch me
For I'll run so far away
That the Sun can never trail me;
Then he will not know the way.

Dashed old Napa o'er the mountains;
Ran and ran like bison run;
Then he slept and when he wakened,
Right beside him stood the Sun.
Fear made Napa's legs to weaken,
And he begged like any coward
While the Sun stood there beside him
Stood there silently and glowered.

"Napa," said the sun, relenting,
"Listen to the words I tell,
As a thief you're very clever
But a mighty fool as well.
For you steal while in my tepee;
Steal from *me* and run and hide.

THE STORIES IN VERSE

Don't you know the world's my tepee;
That it's tall and broad and wide.

"You can never get outside it
If you ran until you died
And if you steal, I'll find you
No matter where you hide.
Steal no more of my belongings
Lest I hurt you bad someday."
Then the Sun went on to Westward
Leaving Napa where he lay.

WHY THE PANTHER WEARS SINGED HAIR
AND IS LEAN AND LONG
(Blackfeet Story)

Once the *Old*-man from a hilltop
Saw ascending o'er the trees
Curling smoke from hidden campfire,
Gently sailing with the breeze.

That is strange—I'll creep upon it;
Creep and see why fire is made;
Growl and scare the merry hunters;
Make them run and be afraid.

Soon he crept where he could listen;
Through the brush saw squirrels at play;
Listened to their merry laughter;
And their chatter bright and gay.

Then he stopped into the open;
Stay—my brothers, you are glad.

THE STORIES IN VERSE

May I play a time among you;
I am old and very sad.

Then they told him of their playing;
How they buried each in turn,
In the ashes of the campfire,
Watching sharp lest hair might burn.

"Good—" he said, "I'll play among you.
Bury me and when I cry
Roll me out but do not burn me;
Give your word and do not lie."

So they buried him in ashes
Till he cried and squirmed about;
Then his brothers, true to promise,
Took some sticks and rolled him out.

Now, I'll bury you my brothers;
All at once and in a row.
(All but one agreed, they tell me,
That one said he had to go.)

In a row he laid his brothers;
Covered them with greatest care,
Stirred the fire and added fuel,
Turned his back and left them there.

Then he made a plate of willows
Scraped away all ash and fire
While a raven soaring o'er him,
Called him forked tongue, or liar.

THE STORIES IN VERSE

Roasted soft the little squirrels
Filled the monstrous willow plate;
Then the *Old*-man always hungry,
Sat him down and ate and ate.

Ate till sleep closed tight his eyelids;
Slept he sound until the dawn;
When he waked great anger seized him
For his plate of squirrels was gone.

Vengeance swore he on the villain;
Strode in search of clew or track;
Found the panther sleeping calmly;
Seized him by the furry back.

Spare me brother, cried the panther.
I was hungry—you were full;
But the *Old*-man mad as rattlers,
Gave his tail a mighty pull.

Placed his foot behind his back-head;
Pulled and stretched the panther out;
Bruised his face against the boulders;
Singed his coat all 'round about.

Now, you sneak, you night marauder;
You can never carry fat,
And as long as time is measured
You must always look like that.

THE STORIES IN VERSE

Once upon the level plain
A deer and antelope
Met beside a water hole,
And, being cousins, spoke.

"I'm faster much than you are
And although you're rather tall,
I'll beat you running now and here;
I'll bet my sack of gall."

"I'll stake you mine against it,"
The deer made quick reply;
"For if you beat me running
You'll surely have to fly."

A race they ran and antelope,
Although he wasn't tall,
Beat the deer upon the plain
And took his sack of gall.

Then said the deer, "If you will come
Back on the hills with me,
I'll run again and beat you;
This ground's too flat for me."

So back they went upon the hills
And bet their dew-claws there.
The deer won from the antelope
And both declared it fair.

THE STORIES IN VERSE

So now the deer wears dew-claws;
The antelope has none;
The deer's without his gall-sack
Because he couldn't run.

WHY THE INDIAN WHIPS THE BERRIES FROM BUSHES

One day, in a pretty river
Napa saw some berries shine.
Thought they grew there in the water;
Grew in clusters red and fine.

In he jumped to pick the berries;
Mussed the water and they fled.
Nearly drowned, the foolish Napa—
When he reached the bank he said,

"Ha, I saw you plain before me,
And I'll wait and watch from here.
Then I'll catch you, cunning berries,
When again you dare appear.

By and by when water settled
And was smooth and clear once more,
There appeared again the berries.
Napa saw them from the shore.

Splash—the fool dived in the water
But the berries were not there.
Gaining shore the berry-seeker
Sat him down to think and stare.

THE STORIES IN VERSE

Suddenly he saw above him
Berry clusters red and fine,
Growing as they do on bushes;
On the streams their shadows shine.

"Ha!" said Napa, "I will show you."
So he broke the limbs away;
Whipped the berries from the branches
Till upon the ground they lay.

"Now," he said unto the berries,
While upon the ground he sat;
"When my people gather berries
They must always do like that."

LEGEND OF THE *OLD*-MAN AND FOX
(A Blackfeet Tale)

"Little Brother," said the *Old*-man
To the *Red*-fox on the hill,
"I am hungry, very hungry,
Can you not a rabbit kill."

"Long the way, my little Brother,
That we journey and I'm old;
You are swift of foot and cunning;
Very cunning I am told."

Said the *Red*-fox, "No, my Brother,
Hard I've tried since morning came,
But the moon is wrong for hunting
Sore am I and very lame.

THE STORIES IN VERSE

"Bad my Medicine and dreaming;
Weak my heart and I'm afraid.
You have wisdom, *Old*-man brother,
Cannot Medicine be made.

"Many snows have known thy foot-prints;
Great the knowledge that is yours;
Knowledge that is fast increasing;
Long thy Medicine endures."

"Listen, Brother," said the *Old*-man,
"I have lost my bow and spear;
Naught have I to use in hunting,
Although buffalo are near.

"Kill them while they lie a-laughing
At your antics and your tail;
Kill them if you'll aid me Brother,
For I know it cannot fail."

Said the Fox, "The season's waning;
Soon the winter will be here.
I will freeze without my clothing;
Freeze and suffer death I fear."

"Ha! 'Tis vanity, my Brother—
'Tis not cold you really fear:
Hair will grow, and in the winter
Meat we'll have and fire to cheer."

"Good—proceed to pull my hair out,"
Said the Fox, "and I will play,

THE STORIES IN VERSE

As you wish before the bison,
But I fear I'll rue the day."

So the *Old*-man plucked his brother;
Leaving but a bunch of hair
On his tail to make him funny;
Left the white tip growing there.

Scarce the west-wind blew to chill him
As before the bulls he danced;
Danced and rolled he as though crazy;
On his hind-legs high he pranced.

"Ere I met thee on the hill-side,
Saw I three of monster size;
Bulls they are and very cunning,
But the *Old*-man too, is wise.

"With my hunting knife I'll slay them:
Slay the three while yet the Sun
Is looking from the Westward
On the deed that I have done.

"Listen well, O little brother;
First I'll pull out all thy hair;
Leave the naked like the white-fish;
Leave your skin all smooth and bare.

"Bare your legs and bare your body;
Bare your tail up *to* the end
Where I'll leave the whitened tassel:
'Twill be funny you depend.

286

THE STORIES IN VERSE

"Then you'll go and dance before them:
Jump and dance and merry be;
Then they'll laugh for you'll be funny;
Queer you'll look unto the three.

"I will hide and watch them laughing,
For I know they're sure to fall;
With their breath so short from laughing,
Then I'll come and kill them all."

Looked the bulls in growing wonder
At the crazy fox and then
Laughed and laughed and laughing harder,
Fell to earth to laugh again.

Lest they rise and cease their laughing,
Danced the Fox the harder still;
Till the *Old*-man crept upon them
From the stones upon the hill.

With his knife he slew the Bison;
Swift he moved without a sound;
Cut their throats and let their blood run;
Let their blood run in the ground.

Then he skinned and dressed the bison;
Worked he hard but as he skinned
Noticed not that from the Northward
Came a gale of freezing wind.

Long he worked nor warmed his fingers;
Spoke no word unto the Fox;

THE STORIES IN VERSE

When he'd finished, lo, his brother
Had been frozen hard as rocks.

The above is a legend told by the Blackfeet—the *Old*-man
being a Great Spirit.

WHY THE BIRCH TREE WEARS SLASHES IN ITS BARK
(Blackfeet Story)

Know you why the birch tree
Wears slashes in its bark;
Heard you not the story?
I'll tell it to you—hark!

Hot it was and summer;
No breeze there was to blow;
Old-man sought the timber
Where tender saplings grow.

"Blow," he said unto a pine tree;
"Bend and break that air may stir."
Spoke he thus to birch and alder;
Bade the wind to break the fir.

Roared the wind among the treetops,
Snapped the saplings in the gale,
Sprang the doe and fawn from cover,
Made the lynx and lion quail.

Bent to earth the slender birches,
Shrieked and swayed as if in pain.
"Break, O! birch, I tell thee;
"I am Chief," he cried again.

THE STORIES IN VERSE

Strove the wind in mighty effort,
But the birches stood the strain;
And to vent his wrath the *Old*-man
Hacked them all with might and main.

With his hunting-knife he hacked them,
Scored their bark and bade them know
That the birch should show the knife-marks
No matter where they grow.

HOW THE MAN FOUND HIS MATE

Once a man was made by Napa—
With the wolves he had to live;
Without mate or fire or weapon—
Took for food, what wolves would give.

Had no robes nor lodge to warm him;
In the winter suffered cold;
Sought the man for Napa's tepee
And to him his troubles told.

"Go," said Napa, "down the river
And a mate and lodge you'll find.
She will make you clothes and love you,
If you're always good and kind.

So the man went down the river
Till he saw a lodge of skin;
From the top a smoke was curling,
And at last he ventured in.

289

THE STORIES IN VERSE

Near the fire there sat a woman
Dressed in deerskin soft and stout.
When she saw him standing naked,
She was mad and pushed him out.

Then the man went on the hillside;
Rolled great rocks upon the lodge;
Knocked it down and tore the lining;
Made the woman run and dodge.

Then she cried and he was sorry;
Helped her set all right again;
Wore a robe and sat beside her;
Both were very happy then.